Adam & Steve

Adam & Steve

a novel

by Craig Chester

Based on the screenplay
by Craig Chester

Celebrating Twenty-Five Years

© 2005 BY AGM MOVIE PRODUCTION LLC. ALL RIGHTS RESERVED.

MANUFACTURED IN THE UNITED STATES OF AMERICA.

THIS TRADE PAPERBACK ORIGINAL IS PUBLISHED BY ALYSON BOOKS,
P.O. BOX 4371, LOS ANGELES, CALIFORNIA 90078-4371.
DISTRIBUTION IN THE UNITED KINGDOM BY TURNAROUND PUBLISHER SERVICES LTD.,
UNIT 3, OLYMPIA TRADING ESTATE, COBURG ROAD, WOOD GREEN,
LONDON N22 6TZ ENGLAND.

FIRST EDITION: JULY 2005

05 06 07 08 09 a 10 9 8 7 6 5 4 3 2 1

ISBN 1-55583-912-6
ISBN-13 978-1-55583-912-3

CIP 2005048211

CREDITS
COVER PHOTOGRAPHY BY AUSTIN WALSH.
COVER DESIGN BY MATT SAMS.

Chapter One

Adam Bernstein never got lucky. But tonight, November 8, 1987, all that was about to change. He had waited all of twenty-one years to make his drinking-age debut in the cavernous wonders of a Manhattan nightclub. Tonight was the night he would unleash himself upon the world.

To create his goth persona, "Rex Havoc," he had spent hours working on his makeup in his NYU dorm room in the Village. He had covered his pimply, modestly handsome face with white greasepaint, which framed two black-smudged eyes. Through these blinking receptacles he would record a night not to be remembered. Dressed in a black tuxedo jacket, black knickers, and a frilly ruffled white shirt, Adam took great pride in his appearance—especially his hair, which was a Medusa-like black ball of fried straw. In high school, Adam had made his first raid on his sister's makeup supply one fateful night after returning from a Cure concert. Inspired by the languidly empowered misfits onstage, Adam took to goth makeup and huge hair with an ardor that might easily be expected from a gay boy with acne from Long Island. Adam's best friend, Rhonda Gernon, was a little younger but slightly more worldly. Morbidly obese and armed with a penchant for fat-deflecting sarcasm, Rhonda wanted nothing more than to find a dark, moody place to write some dark, moody poetry on the night of Adam's twenty-first birthday. She was still living with her parents in the suburban enclave of Montauk, Long Island, where she had been a freshman to Adam's junior in high school. Misfits of the highest order, fat Rhonda and pizza-faced Adam had bonded immediately upon meeting in the geeks' corner of their school's cafeteria. When they became friends, the universe itself sighed a moan of relief. Without each other, they would have found suburbia to be an unbearably scary place indeed. Together they had vowed to leave that place for the big city—as soon after graduation as possible. To celebrate his very important birthday, Adam decided he would rescue his best friend from the tedium of Long Island mall culture and bring her to his favorite big-city spot: Danceteria. Adam's only stipulation: She must also bedeck herself as a goth. It might tarnish his hard-earned reputation to have Rhonda beside him in her usual garb: too-tight sweats with coordinated teddy bears on the chest and left ankle. They had spent the entire day rummaging through East Village thrift stores for the lace and black leotard that would complete Rhonda's new downtown persona. Tonight her girth would be camouflaged in goth. Adam christened her with a new name as well: "Maura Bid, the Notorious O.B.E.S.E."

Once they were inside the packed nightclub, the two wide-eyed newbies quickly realized that the club was not at all what they had expected. Instead of a cool downtown space filled with cool people doing cool things, Danceteria actually seemed to be about dancing. Walking into the colorful, jostling fray was like falling into a giant packet of Skittles. Dancers adorned with every color of the rainbow bounced around them, leaving Rhonda and Adam to stand out like big, black goth thumbs.

"I don't think this is goth night!" Adam yelled over the music.

"This place sucks," Rhonda agreed. Even amid the din, Rhonda's full-throated voice growled.

"Indeed," he replied.

Rhonda stepped away from her friend. "I'm going to the bathroom. There's an idea for a poem I want to write," With that, she stomped off into a sea of colorful, clownish fun. "Beat it!" she yelled, chewing up and spitting out a glamour-puss in her way.

Standing by the stage, Adam did his level best to remain calm and composed despite the odd glances his freakish exterior attracted. He lit a clove cigarette—de rigueur for any good goth—then took a deep breath of the spiced smoke and pushed his way onto the packed dance floor.

"You smell like a Christmas ham," a colorful queen shouted.

Just then, on the stage looming above the packed dance floor, two red curtains flew open and out stormed the Dazzle Dancers. Composed of eight scantily clad men and women with lithe, glistening bodies, the Dazzle Dancers commanded the stage with mock-sexy panache while the pulsating thump of Animotion's "Obsession" deafened the revelers.

In Adam's estimation, the young man fronting the Dazzlers was perhaps the most sexually provocative creature he had ever seen. With a big blond mane of Chippendales hair, the lead dancer in the act was indeed dazzling—and the complete opposite of Adam. In contrast to Adam's uptight snug collar and frilly pantaloons, the go-go boy was completely uninhibited, intoxicating the crowd in randy crotch-gyrating fun.

Adam stood nervously by the stage. Sensing the misfit, Steve—the lead dancer—zeroed in on him and ground his perfect butt in Adam's painted face. Underneath layers of white pancake makeup, a pimply-faced gay Jew from Long Island blushed.

Later, at the bar, Rhonda sat on an overtaxed barstool, its legs straining from her 300-plus pounds. Rhonda was not impressed with the debauched pansexual ambience but did relish the seemingly endless supply of free peanuts. *How could this be? This truly is heaven on Earth,* she thought, echoing the Belinda Carlyle song playing in the background. Adam did his best to keep his composure as Rhonda licked another bowl clean, then sighed contentedly.

"I wanna leave. I don't belong here," Rhonda groaned. Her downcast look caused her chins to multiply.

"Rhonda! It's fun because we're together," Adam said with too much enthusiasm.

"No, it's not," she stated, poker-faced. Adam looked at her, realized she was joking, and laughed. It was common for them to say something awful to each other since they had both recently discovered the concept of sarcasm.

"You know, you should always dress goth. Black is very slimming."

"This place is such a meat market—it's like a Sizzler buffet." Rhonda was known for using food metaphors to describe herself and her situations.

Rhonda turned to address the bartender. "Hey, can we get some more peanuts?" she popped. Leaning over the bar, Rhonda spied the scantily clad Dazzle Dancers at the other end. All of them were chatting brightly and smoking cigarettes.

"Oh, my God. There's that hot Dazzle Dancer," Rhonda announced. Adam turned around and spied the go-go boy who had displayed his wares for Adam. Adam's eyes bulged, then he caught himself and suppressed his attraction.

"Rhonda, what is the opposite of hot?" Adam asked.

"Cold?" Rhonda replied, her mouth full of peanuts.

"No, the opposite of hot is cool, and we are, like, so totally cool."

Adam was so preposterously pretentious. Rhonda tried to imagine ways she could tell him this—without sounding as if she was telling him this. She knew she should put him in his place. Then she remembered that he was her only real friend and decided to accept his imperfections in a way only a true friend could.

"Go talk to him," she said as Adam's gaze drifted back to the Dazzlers. "You might get lucky."

Adam shot Rhonda a sharp look and thought, *How could she have said this?* Rhonda winced at her faux pas.

"Please," Adam said. "I don't even know if he's gay."

Rhonda scrutinized the go-go boy at the other end of the bar.

"Adam, of course he's gay," she concluded. "He's got frosted hair."

Adam rolled his eyes. "George Michael has frosted hair, and he's, like, totally straight."

Rhonda took her goth gay friend's hand and looked directly into his eyes. "Adam, you're twenty-one. You're, like, almost thirty. You have to be more aggressive." Rhonda taking Adam's hand had made an impression in the way that physical gestures of any kind impact young people who are unused to being touched. He softened.

"What do I say?" he whined.

"Just be yourself."

Adam looked sincerely perplexed. "What's that?" he asked.

Rhonda took a powder puff from her purse and began to touch up Adam's makeup. She thought of crimping his already huge hair but realized she couldn't reach the top of his hairdo without climbing onto the barstool.

"Tell him you liked his dancing," she said with a lewd chuckle.

She pointed Adam in the direction of the go-go boy and shoved him toward the end of the bar, where his destiny awaited.

Adam inched toward the group of Dazzle Dancers. The music was loud, but as he approached he began to catch snippets of their conversation. One of the female Dazzlers was topless and obviously proud of her pert, glitter-sprinkled breasts. She was holding court, and Adam stood directly behind her.

"So I'm standing there talking to Keith Haring," the girl said with affected nonchalance, "and this guy totally compared him to Warhol. It was so embarrassing. Keith hates those comparisons, ya know?"

His confidence wavering, Adam looked back at the one person in the universe who believed in him—not only as a human being but also as an object worthy of a go-go boy's affection. But Rhonda wasn't looking at him. She was busily digging through her massive purse to retrieve a lukewarm pork rib she had stashed there for just such an occasion. Adam watched as Rhonda took a large bite. As she chewed, she spied her best friend and gave him an enthusiastic thumbs-up to continue on his mission.

Adam almost froze. How could he possibly make his entrance into a circle of practically nude dancers, all of whom seemed to be speaking a worldly language that was practically foreign to him. He glanced up to see all eight Dazzle Dancers staring at his outfit, except for Steve, the go-go boy, who was staring into Adam's eyes curiously. Adam insides felt like they were sliding down ice.

The bare-breasted Keith Haring habitué rolled her eyes and said, "Well, I guess Bela Lugosi isn't dead after all."

Adam was crushed. His eyes welled up.

"He is dead," he replied. "People like you killed him."

Dejected, Adam returned to his best friend at the other end of Danceteria's bar and took a swig from the margarita she had ordered.

"How did it go?" Rhonda asked cheerily. Barbecue sauce glistened atop her black lipstick.

"I'm such a loser," Adam groaned.

"You are not. Would I be friends with a loser?"

Adam took one look at his morbidly obese friend eating

cold pork in a nightclub and sighed. Just then Adam felt warm breath on the back of his neck.

"Hey!" a trumpet-like voice said behind him.

Adam spun around with a start, betraying his pretentious persona. His margarita flew backward, smashing into the row of colorful wigs on Styrofoam heads that adorned the long shelf behind the bar. Steve loomed over Adam, whose eyes locked on Steve's glistening, glittering pectorals a few inches away.

"Sorry about my friend Cary," Steve said.

Adam was glad he was wearing makeup. He grimaced a forgiving smile. Rhonda chimed in with her best faux-British goth voice.

"Hi!" she said. "I'm Maura Bid and this is Rex Havoc.

Steve took a long look at Adam, drinking him in with dilated pupils as he overpowered the frail boy with sexual energy.

"Cool look, Rex," Steve said. "My last lover was a goth. Are all of you as wild and nasty as he was?"

Adam was stunned but needed to respond. He pulled himself up and assumed a haughty pose. "The night decrees its own appreciations for some mortals treading the river Styx," he proclaimed.

Rhonda looked at Adam. *What the hell did that mean?* Thankfully, Steve was too preoccupied with getting into Adam's pantaloons to notice Adam's verbal crash-and-burn.

"So, you two don't like to dance?" Steve asked as he chewed on ice vigorously.

"Not to this music," Adam chirped as he rolled his eyes.

"Well, it *is* called Danceteria," Steve observed.

Rhonda saw an opening for a joke.

"Ha!" she exclaimed. "More like Dance-a-Queeria!"

Steve and Rhonda burst out laughing. Adam had that feeling he often got when he met boys with Rhonda: that he was being upstaged. Having no investment in the future of

Adam's potential sexual liaisons, Rhonda could actually enjoy herself in situations like this. This was not the case for Adam, who always felt as though he was dying inside whenever cute guys were involved.

He was waiting patiently for the laughter to subside when, suddenly, Rhonda began to choke on the rib she had begun to nibble again. The laughter stopped as all three of them imagined a scenario in which Rhonda dropped dead right there: the Mama Cass of the '80s.

"Is that, like, a rib?" Steve asked innocently as Rhonda recovered.

"Yeah. It's pork, so I try and stretch it into two meals." Rhonda was proud of her amazing powers of self-restraint and felt she could even afford to share. "You want one?" she asked.

Steve recoiled at the idea. "No, thanks," he said. "I don't have much of an appetite, if you get my drift." He swiped a hand across his lightly dusted nose.

Rhonda and Adam stared at Steve with wide eyes.

"Hey, do you guys want a bump?" Steve asked with renewed enthusiasm.

Adam knew this was all wrong. What was he doing talking to this twink covered in body glitter? This guy was totally uncool. He needed to end this silliness now.

"The Bump? Listen, we're goths, okay? We don't dance— we're dead."

Rhonda was certain Adam had blown it. God, he was pretentious, too pretentious to get laid.

Steve moved in closer to them with a conspiratorial look on his face.

"No," he said. "Not disco, a bump of coke. Drugs?"

Rhonda and Adam looked at each other warily. *Should we?*

A few minutes later Rhonda, Adam, and Steve were squeezing into one of the open stalls in the men's bathroom. Rhonda could barely fit her girth into the cubicle. Steve had to crouch atop the toilet. *I shouldn't have had that third bowl of peanuts,* Rhonda thought, blaming her obesity on the makers of salty bar snacks and delectable barbecue sauces.

Rhonda and Adam had never done cocaine before—though once they had boiled Rhonda's mother's nutmeg down to a resin and smoked it. Rhonda hallucinated for five minutes, then wrote poetry for fifteen. Adam hallucinated for ten minutes and cried for five. All in all, it hadn't been a good experience (to that day Adam could not eat pumpkin pie). Rhonda, on the other hand, enjoyed pumpkin pie more than ever.

After producing a key and baggie from his bejeweled knee-high boots, Steve happily plied the two oddballs from Long Island with enough cocaine to curl John Belushi's eyelashes. In fact, Adam thought about John Belushi as he was snorting the white powder. He recalled how much he had laughed while watching *Saturday Night Live* when he was little and how Rhonda and he had paid to see that piece of shit of a movie *Neighbors.* Now here he was six years later, doing cocaine with Rhonda in a New York nightclub. This was it: They were finally grown-up, finally cool.

The effects of the cocaine hit Rhonda first. She felt her teeth go numb—a sensation that wasn't entirely unpleasant for her. Steve had been doing coke all night to give him the confidence and sense of self-centeredness needed to take the stage in a G-string and body glitter. Once the round was finished, they all piled out of the toilet stall, and Steve flitted away to seduce and abandon several hundred other people. Surprisingly, Adam didn't care. Adam didn't care about anything. All he knew was that the cocaine had taken away the insecurities and awkwardness that had plagued his every waking moment for as long as he could remember. He realized that he liked cocaine and wanted nothing more than to impress the glistening messenger who had delivered it to him. But how?

A few moments later Adam and Rhonda stormed the stage where the sexy and practically nude Dazzle Dancers had performed a short while ago. Adam wanted to show Steve that he could also seduce a room with some sexy dance moves. While several hundred people stared at them in shocked disbelief, Adam and Rhonda danced like maniacs on coke—which is exactly what they were.

Grinding her teeth, Rhonda hollered at Adam. "I don't feel anything, do you?"

From their perch on the stage, Adam spied Steve talking to a good-looking partier whom Adam deemed a potential threat. He got an idea and leaned toward his portly friend.

" 'Lucky Star!' " he squeaked.

Adam began mimicking moves from Madonna's "Lucky Star" video. Rhonda eagerly followed Adam's lead, as if she had been born to do this very thing. Suddenly, the depressed girl who wrote poetry in the bathroom vanished, and a jovial chunky chick who loved to dance took her place.

Adam saw that Steve wasn't paying attention to the performances. He lost his footing and his groove.

" 'Borderline!' " he screamed. Rhonda was beginning to sweat profusely.

" 'Dress You Up!' " yelled Rhonda through her coke-induced lockjaw. She and Adam did the appropriate step, ball, change.

The crowd of downtown revelers watched in stunned silence as the two pasty-faced goths bounced around the stage like demonic black Silly Putty. Steve finally noticed the spectacle that was Maura Bid and Rex Havoc.

Rhonda had so much energy, she could have done a hundred jumping jacks on that stage. In a momentary burst of excitement, she flung her fat body across the stage and careened onto Adam. They both tumbled into a heap on the boards, and Adam sprained his wrist in the process. But he didn't care—he was feeling no pain, physical or emotional.

He jumped up and continued his dance seduction for the muscled god who watched from the sidelines.

Steve smiled at Adam. Perhaps he had truly found his meal for the night. In Adam, he saw someone as recklessly uninhibited as himself—or at least as uninhibited as himself on cocaine.

Later, after their energy was spent, Rhonda and Adam stood by the exit, giggling like the giddy patrons they had claimed to despise only a few dance moves earlier. Adam was holding his right wrist, which had been steadily swelling since his tumble. The frilly goth lace cuff of his shirt was becoming increasingly snug. In fact, Adam's entire outfit was beginning to feel uncomfortable. The cocaine made him want to rip off his clothes—which was odd, considering how much he loathed his physique, or lack of one.

Rhonda noticed Adam cradling his wrist.

"I'm so sorry," she said with a laugh.

"That's okay," Adam replied. "At least it's not the same one as last time." They had taken a similar tumble at a Long Island Costco recently when Rhonda tried to reach a shelf of peanut butter. On her way to the floor, she had grabbed Adam's wrist—the one that was now uninjured—and had taken him down with her.

Just then, Steve appeared in the lobby of the club. He was wearing an acid-washed jacket and acid-washed cutoffs with boots that Nancy Sinatra might have worn had she been homosexual in the '80s.

"Hey, Rex!" Steve yelled.

Rhonda and Adam looked at Steve, then turned to each other in a fit of giggles.

"Oh, my God!" Rhonda gasped. "He totally looks like that guy in the A-Ha video."

Adam chuckled. "Well, he can take me on anytime," he said as one of the female Dazzler's sprang from the club into the lobby and briefly claimed Steve's attention.

Rhonda laughed heartily. She loved her friend right now. She loved everything right now. Adam, on the other hand, was falling in love with something else.

"Do you think he has some more cocaine?" Adam wondered, trying to be nonchalant about such grown-up things.

Rhonda was taken aback.

"Oh, my God!" she exclaimed. "You are, like, totally addicted after one bump."

Adam knew she might think this, so he laughed dismissively. He hoped she would think he was having a lark and not ravenously craving more drugs—which he was.

"No, I'm not," he said with a wave of his uninjured hand. "It's not like I thought it would be. It's—fun!"

Rhonda grimaced. "Well, it totally gave me the Hershey squirts," she declared. "I hear they cut it with baby laxative."

Adam didn't miss a beat—he was sharp tonight. "Well, you said you wanted to lose some weight."

Rhonda knew she was busted and laughed at herself. Only her best friend could joke about Rhonda's weight. Though she was physically uncomfortable in her body, she had adopted a sort of fatty pride about her size. She used the defense of having a thyroid deficiency and would continue to rely on this argument until the early '90s, when science proved that overweight people were overweight because they simply ate too much food of the wrong kinds of food.

Adam approached Steve just as the female Dazzler air-kissed her goodbyes. "Hi!" he said with nervous excitement.

Steve leaned into Adam, his glittered tits sparkling.

"Are you okay?" he asked. "That's quite a fall you took."

Embarrassed, Adam brushed off his injury. "I'm fine. Just my wrist..." Adam presented his limp appendage to Steve, who took Adam's hand tenderly. Adam's stomach fluttered with infatuation—or was it the cocaine?

"Where do you live?" Steve asked as he gazed intently into Adam's eyes.

"Brooklyn," Adam replied in a whisper.

Steve was happy to hear this. The gods must want this to happen. "Me too," he said. "Wanna walk across the Brooklyn Bridge and watch the sun come up?"

Of course Adam did, but he was a Scorpio and therefore fiercely loyal, so he wavered.

"Well, I can't just leave my friend Rhonda," he said. Adam's goth persona was now completely gone, and he'd blown Maura Bid's cover too. But none of that mattered. Rhonda, sensing her cue, waved to them from near the exit.

"Good night!" she hollered as she lumbered away. And that was that.

Adam and Steve looked at each other and smiled. They were finally alone.

As Adam and Steve entered the Brooklyn Bridge's pedestrian walkway, the purple blush of sunrise tinged the arches before them. Adam was talking—a lot.

"Yeah, I never get lucky," he said. "You know, that Chet Baker song, 'Everything Happens to Me'? Well, that's my whole family: cursed. But now I've moved out of my parents' house. I'm at NYU and the future's so bright, I gotta wear shades."

As they approached the apex of the bridge, Steve swung Adam around to join him on his favorite spot—a place that afforded a bird's-eye view of lower Manhattan. Steve had come here numerous times to gather his thoughts and rehearse monologues for his acting class. Above the whir of the passing cars and trucks below, Steve could emote dramatically and disturb only passing cyclists.

"I'm at Columbia," he told the willowy goth beauty standing beside him.

"This cocaine is from Colombia?" Adam asked.

"No!" Steve exclaimed. "I'm at Columbia University—

uptown? I'm a theater major. We're doing *The Sound of Music*—I'm up for the Captain." Steve launched into a hyper rendition of the song "Something Good" from the musical.

Perhaps I had a wicked childhood.
Perhaps I had a miserable youth...

Steve did a Rockettes-style leg kick in his Daisy Dukes to impress Adam. "I'm gonna be on Broadway!"

"Wow," Adam said. "Well, don't give up. You obviously have a huge talent. Oh, my god—just kidding!"

"Yeah, my dad's a preacher," Steve said, missing Adam's double entendre. "I grew up singing in church."

"Cool. My dad's a Jew. We don't really sing, unless you count moaning."

Steve suddenly became quite serious. He stared into Adam's eyes in an intense, cokey way.

"You know the whole story of Adam and Eve, and how God took a rib from Adam and made Eve and that's why men need women—to complete them? Well, sometimes I think, *What about me? Who's got my rib?*"

Adam was taken aback by Steve's abrupt shift in tone.

"I don't know," Adam replied, giggling uncomfortably. "Maybe you can borrow one from Cher?" The cocaine made it impossible for him to feel any deep feelings. With cocaine Adam had finally achieved one of his life goals—to become deeply superficial.

Steve took Adam's hand and placed it on his rib cage. "You know what?" Steve said with dilated pupils. "Underneath Rex Havoc lies a beautiful boy."

He pulled Adam closer. Warmed by the golden boy's body, Adam felt safe. He rested his head on Steve's shoulder, and they turned to watch the World Trade Center towers catch the first light of the rising sun.

"Wow," Adam whispered, "Isn't New York beautiful?"

As they entered Adam's dilapidated building at Smith and Ninth Streets, Adam and Steve could barely contain themselves. Sexual energy had been crackling between them since Danceteria. When the door closed behind them and they got into the stairwell, they attacked each other, kissing and groping with reckless abandon away from disapproving eyes. Adam's white face paint was smeared across Steve's face.

They burst through Adam's apartment door, and Steve briefly noted the posters of Morrissey and Cyndi Lauper that adorned the gray walls. Over the lone window, a large purple beach towel served as a makeshift curtain. A single stream of morning sun peeked through a small tear. On the matted shag carpet lay a thin, dingy mattress.

The moment Adam had closed the door, Steve took Adam's keys and produced the small glass vial filled with the magic white powder. He took a snort, then offered Adam one too.

"It's like I've known you my whole life," Steve said as the coke tingled in his willing nostrils.

"Really? It's not just the drugs?" Adam asked as his eyes grew saucer-like.

"Oh, no," Steve replied. "This is *waaay* bigger than drugs."

"Oh, my God, I know!" Adam averred.

Adam felt the coke kick in. He suddenly had the irresistible desire to remove his frilly goth clothing. It was time for Rex to go now. Someone else would replace him, but it wasn't Adam. It was a sex beast. He jumped onto the bed, arms flailing, and flung off his pants and shoes, revealing knee-high black socks.

"When I saw you dancing up there, I knew you were the one," Adam blurted.

Steve joined Adam on the bed, and towered above the crouching Robert Smith look-alike.

"I knew I was the one too," Steve snarled.

"Where have you been my whole life?" Adam asked without irony.

"Looking for you!" Steve declared.

"Here I am!" Adam cried.

Suddenly, Adam's tone changed. He grabbed Steve's thickly muscled legs and gazed up at him.

"I...love you," he said.

It didn't at all seem strange to Adam that he should profess his love to Steve. It seemed right—to both of them.

"I love you too," Steve said.

They embraced for as long as their hyped-up state would allow, which wasn't long. Then Steve jumped off the bed.

"What's your name again?" he asked.

Steve had not told Adam his name either. Unfazed by these omissions, he stripped off his shorts and his jacket, leaving only his glittery knee-high boots. As Steve sauntered into the kitchen to get a glass of much-needed water, Adam marveled at his ass: two muscled globes of manly goodness.

Adam rummaged through Steve's cutoffs to find the vial of cocaine. He took the key to his deadbolt lock to do his first solo bump. At that moment, Adam took off his druggie training wheels. He sat cross-legged at the foot of his bed, doing bump after bump with no notion that he should pace himself. Very quickly, he became almost incomprehensibly stoned. What little self-control he had was by now completely gone.

Steve returned to the living room and stuck an imperious pose before Adam. His naked body glistened with sweat.

Adam did another bump, coughed, and then gazed up at his golden boy.

"You have such an awesome body," he said. "Do you, like, exercise and stuff?"

Steve smiled smugly; he was used to receiving compliments. He reached for the cocaine Adam held and took some for himself.

"Yeah," he said. "I think I'm the only gay man in the world who works out."

Adam did more coke and studied Steve's nakedness with jittery fascination.

"What's that muscle called?" he asked, pointing. "On your arm?" His words rushed out of his mouth in an almost incomprehensible fashion.

Steve looked at Adam coyly and flexed the back of his arm. "Triceps?"

"Oh, yeah," Adam snarled. "Yeah!"

Steve got that Adam wanted a show. And if Steve knew how to do anything, it was how to put on a show.

He flexed his back as he began a manic muscle-pumping pose session.

"Lats…"

He flexed his stomach, smacking his hard six-pack with his meaty paws.

"Abs!"

Adam snorted some more powder. *This is incredible. This guy is so sexy,* he thought. "Quads!" Steve grunted. He had never felt more sexually empowered, and he'd never felt so comfortable with himself and another person than in this moment. Dizzy with excitement (and a belly full of blow), he turned around to show off his best feature.

"Glutes!"

Steve flexed his ass, which morphed into two rock-hard squares. Adam ground his teeth, imagining what he would be doing with this hot, sexy young man in just a few short minutes. After this pose session, they would stick their penises into each other for hours—like crazed gay pigs.

"Oh, my God!" Adam exclaimed. "I am, like, the luckiest guy in the world right now. You are so *effing* hot!"

Steve stepped toward the bed and loomed above Adam, who sat cross-legged on the floor. Steve raised his arms and flexed his biceps in one last triumphant pose.

"Biceps!" Steve growled, like a sexy beast.

Suddenly, Steve's face went from seduction to worry to horror as a baby laxative–induced stream of diarrhea burst forth from his quivering, muscular butt. The single stream of sunlight peeking through Adam's curtain lit *Steve's* stream like a theatrical spotlight. Steve shivered violently, and it was over.

Adam stared wide-eyed at the mess on the floor in front of him. Steve stood motionless, having no coping mechanisms to handle something as deeply humiliating as this, as soul-damaging as this.

As Adam sat on the floor, he tried to conjure ways to make this seem acceptable. Sure, he just saw the guy poop. But why should that ruin the one time Adam had gotten lucky with a guy this hot? Maybe they could take a shower together? That might be kind of sexy. As he was pondering this, he became aware of a warm, wet spot on his upper lip. Bleary-eyed and confused, Adam reached up and touched the spot, smearing the tiny brown fleck that had splattered off his dingy shag carpeting onto his pasty white face.

Realizing this affront, Adam had a singular, involuntary movement in his stomach. He leaned forward and projectile-vomited onto Steve's poop. Adam and Steve had indeed exchanged bodily fluids—but not quite in the way they had intended.

Adam and Steve didn't know what to do. They remained frozen, like statues recovered from an archaeological dig of humiliation. The spell was broken when a tiny puppy emerged from the bathroom, curious to discover the source of these strange new sounds emanating from the living room. Adam saw his little dog, which he had rescued just a week before and had yet to name.

"Puppy, don't look," Adam squeaked. The puppy didn't speak English, but he did smell trouble and wisely made a hasty retreat. Steve regained command of his body. He dropped his arms, took three steps, grabbed his clothes, and slipped out the door, abandoning the situation completely. Adam sat alone in stunned silence. Then, realizing he still had the vial of cocaine, he lifted another bump to his nose and took a self-medicating sniff that would last a very long time.

Chapter Two

Standing at the bar at Pyramid Club, Adam eyed the wall
of booze in front of him. *This was a mistake,* he thought. It
had taken fifteen years of drug and alcohol abuse to create the
hopelessness from which his current six months of sobriety
had sprung. Those six months had been both the hardest and
easiest of his life. They were hard because he realized he had
snorted and imbibed away his youth. Without the numbing
effects of alcohol and drugs, Adam was again face-to-face with
the freak he had felt himself to be all along; the nerd he had
tried so valiantly to extinguish was alive and well. His emotional maturity was frozen in time—like an existential still life
of that fateful night at Danceteria. Adam's sobriety, awkward
as it may be at times, did provide him with stolen moments of
true peace along with a newfound interest in baking.

During these arduous six months, Adam had not ven-
tured far from the safe confines of various AA meetings.
Under the council of sober peers, he had steered clear of
watering holes for fear of "triggers."

"If you hang out in a barbershop, eventually you're going
to get a haircut," they had warned. As he stood nervously at
the bar in Pyramid, Adam almost felt the shears on the back

of his neck. He turned away from the pretty bottles and surveyed the crowd.

"Welcome, welcome to '80s night here at the Pyramid!" Party host Chip Duckett's voice echoed over Animotion's "Obsession" as Adam studied the packed crowd of twenty-somethings. Adam was now thirty-six years old, but since he was still emotionally twenty-one, he felt a vague sense of belonging. As always, his insides and outsides felt out of sync.

Adam studied his sad Diet Coke with lime. Nonalcoholic drinks with limes felt more like alcoholic ones. That tart garnish was all Adam had to make him feel less conspicuous.

On the dance floor a young, adorable twink caught Adam's eye. The twink was doing his best Britney Spears moves to the beat of an '80s classic that wasn't much older than he or Ms. Spears. Adam rolled his eyes.

The twink noticed Adam and busted a few provocative moves. Adam, uncomfortable with his sexuality devoid of coke-strengthened insulation, smiled devilishly; then, in an attempt to rest his arm on the bar, he slipped, causing his Diet Coke to go careening across the bar. The lime landed near a hot young man, who was sneakily snorting coke near the bar.

After some quick apologies, Adam's "sober feet" took him away from this place of temptation and outside to the smoking area, where he could try to remember who he really was.

Since every gay man in the East Village smokes, the patio behind Pyramid was always packed—a carcinogenic can of sardines. Adam waved his way through the cloud of burning tobacco and perched himself in the least smoggy spot he could find. Adam had quit smoking the same day he quit drugs and drink, and he had been clinging desperately to his beloved nicotine patches ever since. Underneath that square inch of reassurance lay complex emotions with which Adam was just beginning to learn to contend.

Suddenly, a large plume of cigarette smoke wafted Adam's way. As it cleared, the twink from the dance floor appeared before Adam, as if by magic.

"Hey, I thought you left!" the twink exclaimed.

Adam regarded the barely legal apparition with wary lust.

"No," Adam replied. "I just came out for some fresh air." Adam coughed as the twink's cigarette smoke swept down his windpipe. Now that he had ingested secondhand smoke, Adam thought that perhaps it would be okay to smoke in a firsthand way—at least he wouldn't be drinking. "But if you can't beat 'em, join 'em, right?" he said. "Can I have a hit of that?"

The twink obliged, handing Adam his fag. Adam smoked it as if it were a joint—with two fingers, like an addict. The twink regarded Adam with a knowing smirk.

"Don't you just love this retro '80s music?" the twink said as Adam exhaled smoke luxuriantly. "Reminds me of slumber parties in grade school." Adam coughed in gagging disapproval. He was way too old to be here. He was in his thirties—for a gay man, that is like being cast in an all-gay remake of *Cocoon.* If the twink was on the prowl for a daddy, he was about to be sorely disappointed because Adam was still a boy—a man-child.

The twink watched with wry amusement as Adam ripped his nicotine patch off his upper arm. Adam felt his blood pressure soar. Surely men *his* age had heart attacks over much less than smoking while on the patch.

"Wow. Someone needs a drink," the twink laughed.

Adam felt a surge of panic. "No, no, no! I'm straight," he blurted.

The twink looked at Adam with arched eyebrows that said, *You're kidding, right?* Adam rephrased: "Sober! Sober…" he explained. The twink took back his cigarette.

"Ew! That sucks ass," the twink said. "I'd hate to be sober.

I don't understand why sober people still get to smoke. Nicotine is such a drug."

Adam felt the need to defend his behavior. "Yeah," he replied, "but nicotine doesn't make me wander through gay bars pinching my nipples and moaning 'pick me, pick me' to hot guys."

The twink took a long drag off his cigarette and gazed at Adam evenly. "Wow. Sounds like you did a lot of crystal— or coke, or crack. But you don't go to Crack Anonymous meetings, because you're just a nice Jewish boy at heart who can only let loose when he's fucked up. You have a lot of guilt, which is why you need drugs to squelch your conscience."

Adam's jaw lowered. "You realize you just said all that out loud, right?" he asked.

The twink lit up. Now he could talk about his favorite subject: himself.

"Yeah," he said, "I'm gonna be an actor, so I pick up on people's personalities. Guys think they're mysterious, but most are just really transparent."

Adam refused to abide this character assassination any longer. Who did this child think he was? How could this twink know anything about life, let alone Adam, at such an early age? Adam snatched the cigarette away from the twink.

"Well, I appreciate the completely superficial deconstruction of my character, but I think I'm a little more complex than you think." Adam chuckled superiorly as he took one last hungry drag on the twink's cigarette.

"Hi! I'm Mary. I used to be a bipolar crack addict, and now I'm just bipolar."

Everyone in the room applauded except for Adam, who sat in the corner of the dingy church basement on Houston Street, his nicotine patch barely reattached.

Mary continued, "Welcome to the midnight Whip That

Crack! fellowship. This meeting is about crack—tonight's topic: crack. But first I'd like to hear from people who are counting days."

Everyone but Adam raised their hands. Mary pointed to a very recent postoperative transsexual. "Rebecca, one day back from the rock," she rasped in a thick Puerto Rican accent.

Everyone clapped, but Adam didn't quite see one day of sobriety as much of an accomplishment from the perspective of his six months, which he felt deserved not only applause but also a shiny new car and six-day cruise.

A timid librarian-type woman excitedly raised her tiny hand. Mary called on her.

"Fiona," the woman announced. "Crackoholic: two days clean and sober."

Mary next called on a young Puerto Rican gangbanger with a bandanna tied around his head. "Orlando, addict," he said with his chin held high. "By the grace of God, I will be two days clean in three days."

Fiona clapped especially hard for Orlando. Adam wondered if perhaps they had been lovers at some point. He imagined them smoking crack and having sex in one of the handicapped stalls at the New York Public Library.

Mary resumed her chairperson duties after the applause subsided.

"Congratulations," she said cheerily. "Now, are there any announcements?"

Suddenly, a jittery biker chick bolted up from her chair. "Yeah," she said. "I think I killed someone today, and I need to talk about it real bad!"

Everyone froze. Adam imagined himself disappearing into the cinder-block walls, becoming a ghost before the biker chick turned him into a real one.

"Oh, dear," Mary mumbled nervously. "Well, we will get to you. But first, let's start with the round-robin."

Mary sat and turned to Adam, encouraging him to begin the sharing portion of the meeting. The biker chick, who needed to talk really badly about murdering someone, slowly sat into her chair, her eyes on Adam, boring evil holes into his *gay fucking face.*

"Uh…hi, I'm Adam and I'm an alcoholic."

The room of addicts bristled. After all, this was a crack meeting—tonight's topic: crack. Adam tried to explain why he belonged there. "Although I mostly did cocaine," he said. "And I did smoke crack back in the '80s—you know, when it was kind of popular?"

The biker chick did not take kindly to this insult. She flipped open her switchblade for Adam's benefit. He regarded her with terror, pleading for his life with his eyes.

"Not that it's not a totally cool drug to be addicted to *now*," he squeaked.

Adam took a deep breath and regrouped. He knew this meeting was about crack. He knew he was a nice Jewish boy at heart who needed drugs to squelch his conscience. But he also needed help. He had learned over the last six months that no matter how crazy he felt, no matter how much he wanted to not feel the jumble of emotions that often paralyzed him, talking about his pain in these twelve-step meetings helped. Somehow they always made him feel better.

"I'm kinda new to this," he said once he felt a little calmer. "I went out to a club tonight, and I thought I could handle it. But I couldn't. I wanted to drink, and if I have a drink, then I want coke. And if I do coke then, well, you know…"

The crack addicts *did* know. They all nodded sympathetically—even the biker chick.

"I just can't go back to that hopelessness again," Adam continued. "I've been chasing that first high for fifteen years and—"

Suddenly—just at the moment when all the sociopolitical, racial, and economic barriers had begun to melt away—

very white, very average Adam's cell phone began to ring. He grimaced as the biker chick pretended to cut off an imaginary penis between her legs in a very unladylike manner. Adam pulled his ringing mobile from his back pocket and nervously answered it. "Hello?" he said, one eye on the biker chick.

Adam heard a familiar sob on the other end of the line. In the background a man with an unidentifiable accent was shouting.

Chapter Three

When Adam burst through the doors of Daisy May's BBQ on Eleventh Avenue, he found his sobbing best friend sitting on the floor. Rhonda was hugging several grease-soaked bags of her drug of choice: food. A Pakistani man in a cowboy shirt loomed over her, hands on his hips.

"You must leave!" he yelled. "There is no crying allowed!"

Adam held his hand up to silence the angry shopkeeper and took charge of the situation.

"Sir! Please!" he said. He knelt on the floor next to his friend of twenty years who through Overeaters Anonymous had lost nearly 200 pounds over the course of the last year. Rhonda looked pleadingly to Adam as she held a sauce-smothered pork rib precariously close to her quivering mouth.

"Oh, Adam!" she cried. "I'm allowed to have my feelings. Feelings aren't a crime."

Adam knew this was an important moment. As a fellow addict, he knew Rhonda was on the precipice of a very tall building—or rather, a very tall rib joint—and needed to be talked down.

"Of course not," Adam said soothingly. "Of course feelings aren't a crime. Now, come on, honey, give me the rib."

"I want it! I *want it!*" Rhonda screamed. The struggle inside her was immense.

Adam's face grew stern. "No, you don't!" he said. "That is your disease talking. Now, play the tape through. You eat everything on the menu, then what happens?

Something clicked in Rhonda. Having Adam in front of her had reminded her of who she really was.

"I'll just want more?" she squeaked. Suddenly, the room began to come back into focus as her eyes dried slightly. "One is too many, and a thousand never enough."

Adam had done well. He knew it wouldn't help for him to grab the rib from Rhonda. She had to make the choice herself to save her own life.

"Now, put the rib in the bag," Adam said, gently.

Rhonda begrudgingly dropped the tasty, blubbery pork into the bag Adam held before her. Adam smiled. He took Rhonda's sticky hands in his and helped her to her feet.

Rhonda took a deep breath. The spell was broken.

"Wow. That was close," Rhonda said. She immediately did a ninth step by making amends to her fellow patrons. "I'm sorry, everyone. I'm a food addict."

The Pakistani proprietor looked on disapprovingly. "You Americans have so much food, you get addicted."

It was nearly three A.M. when Rhonda and Adam slid into a booth at Howard Johnson's in Times Square. They were both burned-out, burdened by their massive problems. The blasé façades they had tried so hard to perfect as young adults had now become effortless responses to reality. Still, they had each other. And at three A.M. in a town filled with booze and food, true friendship goes a long way.

A few minutes later, the waiter brought over nachos and a martini. He placed the martini in front of Adam and the nachos in front of Rhonda. The waiter stepped away, and they both stared at their respective poisons for a moment. Then, sighing, they switched items. Adam scooped the Mexicanized American cheese onto a chip.

"So, what triggered this whole thing?" he asked.

Rhonda gave Adam a look that was even drier than the martini she sipped.

"That movie *Babe*," she said. "I know he's cute and everything, but I wanted to climb into the TV set and eat him with apple sauce."

Adam nodded as he scraped a mountain of sour cream off a chip. "You should have gone to a meeting," he said.

Rhonda narrowed her eyes. "There are no fatty meetings at midnight, unlike you AA'ers," she said.

Adam sighed. "Well, it must be in the air," he said. "I almost fell off the wagon tonight too. This twink totally made me want to drink."

Rhonda shook her head, lost in her own thoughts. "God. What happened to me?" she mused. "I used to be so much more fun before I got thin." The warmth of the vodka soothed her hunger. Food addicts usually avoided alcohol (due to the carbohydrates and tendency to lower inhibitions), but tonight Rhonda thought one drink in the company of Adam would be okay, considering the alternative.

Adam gave Rhonda a disbelieving look. "Fun? You broke the axle of a cab. You fell through a subway grate, broke both legs, and still finished the hot dog you were holding."

Rhonda looked at Adam blankly. "My point exactly."

Adam pushed the plate away and searched for his wallet. "Ugh. It's so late," he said. "I gotta get home. Burt is going to be so mad at me."

Rhonda rolled her eyes. "God, you are *so* codependent with him."

"No, I'm not. Tomorrow is his birthday," Adam said, looking hurt.

Rhonda crossed her arms and leaned back. "Don't tell me. You're making him a cake again?"

Adam plucked a twenty from his wallet and shot Rhonda a defiant look. Rhonda and Burt often wrestled for Adam's heart. He often wondered if her critical feelings about his relationship with Burt stemmed from jealousy or genuine best-friend concern.

"Don't lecture me," he said with mock rage. "I like doing cute little things for him. He makes me happy."

Rhonda arched her eyebrows.

"I *love* him," Adam said with a mischievous grin.

Chapter Four

The next day was full of birthday merriment. Adam had spent forty dollars—a lot of money—on Burt's big day. After Adam quit getting high, he had taken a city job doing bird-watching tours in Central Park. While the pay was not so great, it was a sober line of work for someone who was slowly putting his life back together.

Adam had bustled around Hell's Kitchen that morning, buying party hats, candles, a few gifts, and all the ingredients he would need to make a cake from scratch. Adam's mother had always expressed her love through food, and her son had inherited a belly full of people-pleasing tendencies in the process. The only problem was that Burt was not a person. Burt was Adam's dog.

Covered in batter and flour, Adam set his completed masterpiece in front of Burt, who sat patiently at the table with a party hat on his furry head. Adam leaned down next to Burt and lit the fifteen candles stuck in the cake. Adam smiled—he had done well. Before he blew out Burt's candles, he remembered the most important part of any birthday celebration.

"Make a wish," he told Burt. In Adam's mind, dogs

possessed all the same needs and desires as humans. Even dogs had dreams they hoped might come true. After a moment Adam blew out Burt's candles. Burt's wish was to eat an entire strawberry cake—and his dream was about to become true.

Later, as Adam cleaned up, he glanced down at Burt, who lay on the floor with his face covered in pink frosting. Burt's fat belly rose and fell as he snored gently, the object of Adam's confection.

The phone rang, jarring Adam from his reverie and bringing him back to his kitchen, which looked like Betty Crocker herself had committed an act of terrorism. Flour, sugar, and eggshells littered the counter and floor.

"Hey, honey," Rhonda chirped when Adam answered the phone. "I just wanted to call and wish you-know-whom a happy Burt-day." She was standing backstage at her current place of employment: Lou's Laf Attax, a bottom-of-the-barrel comedy club located in a former adult movie theater in Times Square.

Adam sighed. "Well, I'd put him on the phone, but he's in a 'cake hole.' I should be reported to the humane society."

"Oh, please," Rhonda said. I've eaten more than that in one sitting. Remember my sister's wedding cake? She's still mad she didn't get a piece."

Adam *did* remember—almost. He had been in a champagne-induced blackout by the end of the wedding. "And besides," Rhonda continued, "one of the many advantages of being a dog is that you get to eat like a pig."

Just then Lou—the sleazy, pompadoured owner and emcee of the club—approached Rhonda. "Hey, fatso! Ready to go on?" he grunted lewdly. Lou pretended to stick a penis into his mouth and pushed his tongue into cheek to complete the obscene gesture. He laughed and ambled onto the stage as Rhonda rolled her eyes.

"Speaking of pigs," she whispered into her phone. "Lou

just propositioned me again. He's desperate *and* serious."

Adam made gagging sounds.

"Ew, Lou: the other white meat," he said. "Well, at least you're getting sexually harassed. The closest I've been to man since I got sober is the ten-inch salami in my fridge."

From the stage Lou surveyed the four people who occupied his run-down establishment that afternoon. Miranda, perhaps the worst waitress in the world, hobbled about, surreptitiously sipping her customers' already watered-down booze.

Rhonda peeked through the curtain, waiting for her cue as Lou launched into his very cold warm-up routine.

"The audiences have been really tough lately," she told Adam," and I'm sweatin' like Whitney Houston going through customs."

Adam decided to broach a touchy subject.

"You know, honey," he said gently, "you might want to think about rewriting some of your material—you know, since you lost all the weight?"

Although Rhonda knew she was no longer obese, she couldn't incorporate the fact of her skinniness skinny fact into her current perception of herself. Her denial was always strongest right before she walked onto the stage.

"What are you talking about?" she asked sincerely.

Lou wrapped up his introduction of his formerly fat comic by spinning the lyrics of a Beach Boys song to fit his appalling personality. "Help me, Rhonda, yeah! Get her out of my—pants!"

Rhonda gasped as she listened to Lou's pathetic warblings.

"Oh, shit, he's singing the song," she said. "That's my cue."

Rhonda abruptly hung up on Adam, which was perfectly acceptable to both of them. They had been friends so long, they were way past hello or goodbye.

"Ladies and Gentleman, I give you Rhonda Gernon and her fabulous fun bags!"

Lou left the stage to Rhonda. She still stood like a fat girl—legs spread, shoulders slouched. No one clapped; the patrons were much too inebriated to notice other people.

Rhonda put on her comedy face. "Okay, I know what you're thinking. Doesn't she have a pretty face? And what a personality. If only I didn't get my dresses made by Omar the Tentmaker."

The silence was thick and heavy, like a fog. But there was one person laughing—Rhonda. She found her own jokes so hilarious, she often cracked herself up.

"I'm so fat, I eat with a forklift," she chuckled. "I'm so fat, when I back up, my ass beeps." Rhonda laughed until her side ached.

She was no longer fat, but she was definitely still jolly.

Thinking about Rhonda's stand-up routine had made Adam hungry. Climbing onto his much-abused mattress and box springs, he placed the ten-inch salami on a cutting board and decided to spend the afternoon doing something he liked quite a bit—watching TV. Eating salami in bed was perhaps the most solitary act a single person could ever do. If bad breath fell in the forest of Adam's life, it would not make a scent, since no one was ever around to smell it.

As he turned on the TV, Burt jumped on the bed. Patriotic music came blaring through the speakers as the screen displayed the image of a serving plate featuring a bald eagle soaring over lower Manhattan. A woman's voice with a Southern accent narrated the infomercial.

"This 9/11 commemorative plate features the American bald eagle in all her majestic glory, a single cubic zirconium tear emblazoned on her proud face. Fashioned from actual ceramic chips recovered from Ground Zero, this limited-edition keepsake will make a fitting addition to your other 9/11 collectibles."

Adam recoiled from this blatant commercialization of the tragedy. Still, it was captivating as a car wreck. He couldn't take his eyes off the TV. As Adam sliced through a particularly hard spot of his salami, the knife slipped, bouncing off his dog's rib cage. Adam lifted the bloody knife up to his face as his heart leaped into his throat.

Chapter Five

Adam burst through the doors of his apartment building onto the sidewalk, a bleeding Burt in his arms. Knowing that seconds mattered, he ran. He ran as fast as his legs could carry him up Tenth Avenue to the closest hospital—St. Luke's Roosevelt.

As Adam approached the massive building, he couldn't remember where the emergency entrance was. He had OD'd several years ago and still had a hazy memory of this place, but he couldn't remember the layout. Finally, he spotted signs leading him to his dog's salvation. Sweating and exhausted, Adam burst through the doors to the ER, screaming and crying, "Help! Oh, my God—somebody *help* me!"

It took Adam a moment to realize that he had left his apartment building in only a T-shirt, underwear, and flip-flops. Saving Burt was much more important than a social convention such as, say, pants. A large female orderly standing at the nurses' station cleared her throat loudly, and people with semiserious injuries stared at Adam in disbelief.

"Sir," the orderly said. "Animals are not allowed here: hospital policy."

Adam looked at her in stunned disbelief. "What? What

do you mean, hospital policy?" he demanded.

"You're gonna have to keep your voice down, sir," the orderly said, parking her fists on her wide hips. "Now, there is a very good animal hospital over on First Avenue."

Adam felt himself coming undone. He had come so far to save his baby's life—why wouldn't they help him? He was defiant. A mother's love can lift cars; maybe it could lift the sympathies of large orderlies too? "But I am not on First Avenue. I'm on Tenth Avenue, and there is medical equipment here, and he has a heart and a brain and lungs just like a normal person," Adam cried as he clutched the forty-pound terrier mix in his arms. The orderly was not sympathetic to Adam's disorderly public display of affection. She motioned to a nearby security guard, who stealthily moved toward the wide-eyed, weeping gay man in his skivvies.

"Sir, please come with me," the security guard said.

Adam realized he needed to change tactics.

"No, I'm sorry. I'll be quiet. I'm sorry, if you could just help him. There was an accident—I stabbed him. I stabbed him accidentally."

The people in the waiting area gasped. Several grabbed their children in horror. Upon hearing this new information, the orderly knew just what to do. She picked up the phone and dialed the psych ward.

"We've got another dog stabber down here," she said into the receiver.

A few moments later a handsome doctor in a lab coat stepped into the drama in the ER waiting room. Adam had slumped to the floor. He was clutching Burt's limp body and crying. He had refused to budge until someone helped his dog.

The security guard moved in to drag Adam and Burt away. Adam twisted away from him and said, "This is not an animal! This is my child! I'm a single gay man in New

York City, don't you understand? I might as well have given birth to him."

The handsome doctor was Steve, the former Dazzle Dancer and party pooper. In the years since 1987, he had completely reinvented himself. Calm, collected, and devoid of any rough edges, Steve took in the messy scenario unfolding before him. He was prepared to deal with just another lunatic off the street, but when he heard Adam out himself as a gay man with a dog-child, he realized that Adam was not insane, just perhaps a little sad. Steve regarded the security guard. "Ron, it's okay. Sir, bring the dog on back."

Everyone in the waiting room was shocked that this doctor had actually taken pity on the dog stabber from hell. But no one was more shocked than Adam. He slowly got to his feet and gratefully stepped toward Burt's savior.

As Adam approached Steve, there was no thought in either man's mind that he had met the other fifteen years ago. Lifetimes had passed since then. The world had changed as much as they had. The Internet and cell phones had appeared; presidents had been voted in and out of office; the specter of AIDS had diminished, at least in the United States and Europe. Adam took in Steve's benevolent face and turned back to the gaping crowd and the surly medical staff who had done nothing to try to save Burt's life. "At least there is still one caring person left in the medical establishment," Adam exclaimed.

A half hour later Adam sat in a private room, his face in his hands, waiting for Steve to return with news of his "child's" medical condition. Adam knew what it was like to deal with doctors. He had grown up in a world filled with physical injuries, but the difference these days was that Adam had nothing with which to numb himself. He considered how he would deal with news of Burt's death. He was preparing himself for just such news when Steve entered, covered from head to toe in surgical scrubs. Steve was holding X-rays, which he placed on a light board.

He mumbled something unintelligible underneath his surgical mask.

"I can't hear you," Adam said, desperate to hear the news.

Steve pulled down his mask.

"Oh, sorry," he said. "Your dog has a bruised rib that the knife must have grazed as it entered. There's a little clouding around the abdomen, which you would expect in any puncture wound."

Adam gasped. "Is he bleeding internally?" he asked.

"A little but nothing life threatening," Steve replied.

Adam lit up like the Christmas tree at Rockefeller Center. He leaped to his feet and hugged the germphobic doctor with glee. "Thank you. Thank you so much," he said. "Oh, my God. I can't thank you enough for helping us."

Adam smiled at Steve through a snotty nose. Steve was alternately horrified and touched.

"That's quite all right," he said. "Would you like to see him now?"

Adam nodded and followed Steve to the examining room. Adam strolled through the hospital in his underwear, heedless of the fact that people might laugh at him or judge him. Adam's lack of self-consciousness was completely foreign to Steve. He also found it strangely attractive.

Burt's tail began wagging when he heard his daddy's voice in the hallway. He sat up when Adam entered the room—he had a bright, new bandage wrapped around his middle. Adam rushed over, sat next to Burt, and hugged him dearly. Steve watched them—a little family of two.

"Well, I have to say that his *fat* protected him from that knife," Steve said, "although in the long run you might want to put him on a diet."

"Yeah, I don't know why he's so fat," Adam said. He scratched Burt's chin, trying to act nonchalant. He knew he was responsible for his dog's obesity. He knew he overfed him, and now he had stabbed him. Adam briefly wondered if Munchausen by Proxy syndrome happens between owners and their dogs. He reached out his hand. "I'm Adam, by the way."

Steve offered his own hand. "I'm Doctor Hicks," he replied. He removed his surgical cap. "Steven."

They smiled at each other, and a tingle of energy passed between them.

"Are you a veterinarian?" Adam asked.

"No," Steve replied, "I run outpatient mental health services here. I wanted to be a veterinarian—I actually love animals."

"Why didn't you?" Adam asked.

"I couldn't stand the idea of dealing with neurotic pet owners on a daily basis." Adam smirked, and Steve realized what had just flown out of his mouth. It was not like him to be this unself-conscious in front of any human being. He immediately recanted. "Sorry," he said.

Adam knew he had an opening. "That's okay," he said. "It is sad how people attribute human qualities to animals instead of just eating their flesh or wearing their fur."

Steve smiled. He was fascinated. He wanted to know this weird guy.

"So, Adam, let's talk about you," he said.

"Me?" Adam replied, flirty.

"Yes, do you want to tell me what drove you to stab your dog?"

Adam gulped. "Look, it was an accident," he said. "I was eating a salami, this big ten-inch…" Steve arched his eyebrows as Adam blushed. "I love this dog more than I love myself," Adam continued, "more than I love my life. I know that may sound dumb, but I'm not crazy."

Steve folded his arms and looked at Adam intensely. "I know you're not crazy," he said. "Actually, it's refreshing to see a person love something or someone that much."

Adam looked at Steve. He suddenly felt very *seen* by Steve. "Oh."

The mood was broken when an orderly wheeled a loud, screaming homeless woman into the room. The woman was yelling at her crotch.

Adam pointed and said, "Now, *that's* crazy."

Steve sighed and nodded. "Yep," he said. "Welcome to my world."

And off Steve went to tend to the crazy lady. Adam watched him go. Steve had behaved like a true gentleman, a real hero.

For the first time in his life, Steve took note of people on the street with their dogs while he was on his way home from work. He wondered about the special bond between canines and Homo sapiens and tried to imagine having a dog in his life or, for that matter, a child. Steve had always harbored dreams of fatherhood, of marriage and the white picket-fence ideal. Walking through the West Village, he wondered how he would react if something or someone he loved were seriously hurt. Working in a Manhattan psych ward had hardened him, but in all his years he had never seen the kind of selfless concern that Adam demonstrated that day. Most loved ones of sick people seemed preoccupied with how their loved one's illness affects *them.* But Adam seemed to have no concern for himself whatsoever. He had been completely unself-conscious standing in a busy waiting room, crying in his underwear for all to see. He loved his dog—more than he loved himself? That notion struck Steve as psychologically unsound, but something about Adam made sense. Steve envied the depth of Adam's feelings for Burt.

As Steve approached his apartment building on Grove Street, he had a revelation. He did have a dog. His dog was Michael, a straight, unemployed thirty-five-year-old actor who lived on Steve's couch. Michael had all the attributes of a dog—mainly his complete and utter dependence on Steve. Five years ago Michael had been thrown out of his rent-controlled apartment in the East Village, and he'd asked his friend Steve if he could crash at his place. Michael had been living on Steve's couch ever since. Michael never left the apartment—ever. He required no walking, though, and he was toilet trained, unlike some other pets.

Steve entered his loft and sorted through the mail. His apartment was like something out of a magazine. Tasteful and minimalist, his loft consisted of a large living area that flowed into an immaculately marbled kitchen. Steve's private domain was not unlike the hospital where he worked: It was clean, sterile, and sanitized. A large beige sectional occupied the middle of the living area, where Michael camped out. Several Japanese screen dividers between the couch and the bedroom provided a modicum of privacy for each roommate. In truth, privacy was never an issue for the bachelors since neither of them ever brought anyone home to spend the night.

Steve moved toward the sectional, his nose in the mail, as Michael shouted over the loud beeps and whistles emanating from the television set, where he was playing a video game.

"Hey, gay doctor roommate," Michael cried. "Tough day at the orifice?" Steve often recounted to Michael the stories of the loonies and crackpots he had seen at the ER.

"Oh, the usual," Steve said. "A woman who thinks God speaks through her vagina."

Michael's ears pricked up, and he looked at Steve with wide eyes. "Oh, my God," he said. "Wait! Paulie?"

Steve pulled his nose out of the mail as Michael stared at him expectantly.

"Oh, Michael. No, no, no," Steve said, shaking his head.

"Yeah, she's, like, five foot eight, blond, thirties—goes by the handle 'Stone Pillow' on the street?"

This information confirmed Steve's worst fears. He had carefully assessed the mental state of Stone Pillow to try to find a way to silence the voice of Jesus that called out to her from between her legs. He was appalled. Steve grabbed the remote control to the television and muted its annoying beeping.

"Michael, you had sex with a psychotic homeless woman?" Steve exclaimed, slack-jawed.

Michael realized his behavior did seem questionable, so he tried to explain.

"It was kinda sweet, actually," he said. "Not the way you're making it sound." Steve looked at his roommate in disbelief, then walked away, loosening his tie. Michael, who never knew when to quit, forged ahead. "It was very intimate," he said. "We actually cuddled a lot."

"She was probably cold," Steve blurted from his side of the loft.

A wounded, pious look stole across Michael's face. "You know, homeless people have needs—they need love like other folks! I actually helped her, provided a service for her." Michael mused for a moment on the enormity of his compassion. "For five minutes her vagina stopped talking to her."

It was not unusual for Steve and Michael to recount their numerous sexual conquests with each other. Steve's righteous indignation about Michael's latest conquest had less to do with the fact Paulie was homeless and insane and more to do with the fact that Michael had stuck it in someone *dirty.* Someone unclean.

Steve stood in the doorway of the bathroom and shouted, "Michael! I am going to take a shower—for both of us."

Chapter Six

Uptown, Adam sat on the edge of his bed, the very bed where he had stabbed his dog-child, and fed Burt his favorite food item: peanut butter. Rhonda was cleaning Adam's messy apartment by rote—something she did every time she visited. Adam did not have the gay gene that gives gay men the innate ability to dress stylishly and decorate their homes tastefully. Most of Adam's furniture had once existed as garbage he found on the sidewalks of Hell's Kitchen: Adam was poor. That the handsome doctor Steve had not only saved Burt but also persuaded the hospital to waive the pricey bill for ER admittance had left a strong impression on Adam.

"He was like this total knight in shining armor—and sweet. And cute!" Adam said giddily as he let Burt lick the peanut butter off a spoon. Rhonda liked the sound of this. She was desperately trying to find Adam a boyfriend, not just because she loved Adam dearly but because she knew he needed to be loved in a way that was not just platonic. Rhonda, however, was completely unable to see herself in an intimate relationship with any man. Her romantic ambitions for Adam were the means for her to soothe her own thwarted desire for love.

"Wow, that's so amazing," she called from the kitchen. "Your mom would be happy for you, marrying a nice doctor. Is he Jewish?"

This hadn't even occurred to Adam. He remembered Steve's wavy, beautiful blond hair. "I don't think so," he said. "Whatever, I'll never see him again—unless I go insane." Adam pondered this prospect. He imagined that when he eventually did go insane—and he most likely would—he would return to the ER to find Steve, who would decide that Adam was not insane after all, just misunderstood. Then Steve would rip off Adam's straitjacket and make passionate love to him right then and there on a gurney.

Rhonda wandered in from the kitchen and sat on the bed next to Adam. Her voice had changed, as if she was reprimanding an old woman for shoplifting. "Adam," she said. "We're in our thirties. We're almost forty. You need to be more aggressive. Why don't you go back to the hospital?"

Adam recoiled in horror at the idea of pursuing, well, anyone—let alone someone as smart and handsome and successful as Steve. "No," he said. "He already thinks I'm a crazy pet person."

Adam raised the spoon covered with dog-slobbery peanut butter to his mouth and licked it clean as Rhonda stared at him blankly.

Freshly showered, Steve stood in his bedroom in an expensive terry cloth robe. Michael lounged on the bed as Steve ironed his shorts and tank top in preparation for the gym.

"You're the only person I know who showers before the gym," Michael mused sleepily.

"Well, I need to blow off some steam," Steve said as steam rose from the tube socks on the ironing board.

"Among other things," Michael cracked.

"That's right," Steve replied with a lewd grin.

Michael writhed on Steve's multithousand-thread-count sheets and sighed. "God, you gay guys are so lucky. You get to make love and connect with someone different every night."

Steve nodded his agreement as he inspected his socks for wrinkles.

"If straight women were as promiscuous as you," Michael said, "there'd be orgies in the street."

"Well, thanks to you, there already are," Steve observed drily.

Michael snorted, sat up, and slapped Steve's bed hard. "Nah. I brought Stone Pillow back here."

Steve was repulsed by the idea that Michael had had five minutes of sex with dirty, stinky Paulie on his not-at-all-stony pillows. Michael arose and slapped his free ride on the back. "Well, have fun having gay anonymous sex in the low-self-esteem room."

Michael lumbered back to the living room and plopped down on the couch, shoving Doritos into his mouth as if by reflex. Steve watched Michael through the translucent room dividers. He thought about the dog guy.

The gym that Steve worked out in resembled most other gyms where upwardly mobile, fastidiously plucked and waxed gay men work out. Thumping house music blared over the speakers, providing the perfect soundtrack to the bumping and grinding seduction that masqueraded as exercise. Steve had an amazing body—perhaps the only thing left over from his previous incarnation as a Dazzle Dancer—and the years had only made him sexier as he grew into his naturally manly features. Steve knew he was hot, and it never occurred to him that someone might not reciprocate his sexual advances. He used sex as a tool to help him feel good about himself. His sexuality was intricately tied to his need to control his own life and body; his body was his main form of currency in a gay community that traded in good looks.

After his workout, Steve stood at the juice bar of his gym, lost in thought, when suddenly he felt eyes on him. He turned and saw the twink Adam had met earlier. The twink was wearing a T-shirt that said SHUT UP, BITCH!

"Hey, you're hot," the twink remarked. "I wish I had your body but, like, with my face."

Steve rolled his eyes at the twenty-one-year-old and downed his wheat grass. "I wish you did too," he said drily.

The twink ignored this and continued, "Wow. Don't you just love this gym? Feels so good to sweat out the Tina, you know?" Steve was appalled at the mention of Tina—slang for the gay party drug crystal methamphetamine. He had spent a lot of his time counseling patients whose crystal abuse had led to schizophrenia-like delusions. Thank God he'd given up drugs when he left Columbia's theater program for medical school—if only everyone knew how bad drugs were for them.

"Oh, no, I don't actually," Steve said. "I don't use drugs, and neither should you."

The twink smiled. He had him.

"Ah. Sounds like someone had a bad experience with drugs," he said.

Steve felt his ears turn red. "Excuse me?"

The twink gently placed his warm hand on Steve's well-muscled shoulder.

"It's okay. I'm just really observant. I notice things that other guys might not."

Despite himself, Steve was intrigued. "Is that so?"

"Yeah. I'm gonna be an actor, so I pick up on people's personalities. You don't do drugs because you have what I like to call control issues. You're, like, totally afraid of losing control of your body and letting someone see you in a less-than-perfect light—unless it has to do with sex, and then you can completely cut loose and..."

Moments later Steve and the twink were in a shower stall,

sloppily kissing each other behind a closed curtain. Steve had sex in this stall nearly every night. The gym showers afforded him quick and semiprivate hot sex as well as the chance to clean himself of the dirty, *dirty* men he had sex with. For Steve, soap was an aphrodisiac. Soap commercials on TV often made him hard beneath his tailored slacks. The twink had made Steve angry, and Steve's sexual assignations were always tinged with irritation. He pushed the twink against the shower stall, filled his hands with shower gel, and washed a confused but happy twink from head to toe.

After they were done, the twink did the one thing Steve hated most in his tricks—he talked. A lot. He talked and talked and talked about his acting classes, his life, his family. Like most twenty-one-year-olds, the twink assumed he knew everything there was about life. The twink looked at older gay men and thought, *I won't make the same mistakes you have. I'm smarter than that.* What the twink didn't know was that every younger generation thinks exactly the same thing and makes the same mistakes because they don't realize that being smart does not protect anyone from life's steady progress toward eventual humility.

As Steve and the twink left the gym, the twink grabbed his crotch.

"Ow!" he exclaimed loudly. "I think you got soap in my pee hole." A mortified Steve escorted him away from shocked gym members at the front desk.

As Steve and the twink stepped out onto Eighth Avenue, Steve noticed a man with a terrier-mix dog standing outside the gym. Steve lit up and approached the man, excited to see Adam again.

"Hey," he said. Steve deflated, however, when the man turned around, revealing himself to be someone other than Adam. Steve quickly apologized and begged off as the twink caught up with him, dangling on Steve like a tweaking koala bear.

"Ew! Dogs are so gross," the twink exclaimed. Steve winced and pushed the twink away. "How can you love something that shits right in front of you?"

After he had waved off his unwanted companion, Steve stood on Eighth Avenue for a moment and looked up at the Chelsea sky. He thought about Adam—about how unusual and messy he was and about the love for he had for his dog.

When Adam got sober six months ago, he had faced a quandary. He had received an eviction notice from his Hell's Kitchen landlord, he had used up his unemployment compensation, and his loving parents had begun to wonder why he never seemed to be able to make ends meet. For years he had survived by temping in corporate law firms in Midtown Manhattan. Growing up, Adam had wanted very much to be a lawyer. He was that rare exception—a Jewish boy who actually wanted for himself the career his parents wanted for him. He had grown up unlucky, and this had endowed him with a remarkable empathy for others and their predicaments. Adam was a sensitive, emotional man who had never acquired the protective armor that many gay men use to face the world. He felt everything very intensely and had only been able to confront the world under the influence of the emotional numbing power of drugs and alcohol. But the very substances that lent him a thick skin had also robbed him of his ambition and dreams. Before he knew it, he was a fully grown man with no history—unlike most thirty-six-year-olds, who were in the middle of their careers.

Having burned his bridges at most of the firms where he worked due to tardiness and absenteeism, Adam was unemployable for his first ninety days sober. On day ninety-one, however, a friend in Alcoholics Anonymous helped him land the perfect job for an overly sensitive, newly sober gay man— running a bird-watching tour in Central Park.

Adam liked his new job. It allowed him to be in nature—

something he'd never appreciated, and the humility it inspired was good for his sobriety. The job forced him to get up early each day, and his nights were free for meetings and coffee after meetings.

A week after Burt's stabbing, Adam showed up for work feeling particularly optimistic. For some reason, as he dressed in his park ranger uniform, he felt the day was special. Perhaps it was because it was early May and the park was filled with happy New Yorkers thawing out from winter, or perhaps it was because he was reading a self-help book called *The Drama of the Gifted Child*. Or more likely, it was because Adam was finally glimpsing happiness for the first time in his life. He felt hopeful. It was, after all, spring.

Adam led his clutch of tourists through the park—they were the usual maladjusted group of misfits who might take an interest in watching birds. Most bird-watchers tended to be older, something that frustrated Adam since their elephant-like reflexes often inhibited their ability to quickly grab the binoculars hanging around their necks. But that day there was one bird-watcher who was not old. A man dressed in survivalist gear, complete with camouflage makeup, trailed the pack of twenty or so elderly tourists. Adam took note of him but wrote him off as just another New York nut job. Most New Yorkers are familiar with the species.

Adam stopped and faced the tourists. Just then, he saw a beautiful bird fly onto a perch in a tree just behind them.

"Oh! Everyone grab your binoculars. We have a North American White—"

The elderly tourists turned to face the tree behind them just as Adam spied, in the bushes below the tree, two men engaged in fellatio.

An elderly woman finished Adam's sentence.

"Swallow?"

Adam gagged. So did the gay man on his knees.

"Uh—okay. Uh, everyone out of the Rambles. Yeah, the

bird flew away—nothing to see over there." Adam nearly had to drag away each bird-watcher individually before he could coax the group to turn away from viewing the blow job and follow him farther down the path.

Just then the survivalist approached Adam. "Excuse me," he said.

Adam stopped and stared at the man, who appeared to be in his thirties. He spoke in a thick Southern accent and had big, crazy eyes that bugged out slightly.

"Could you eat any of these birds if you had to—you know, like if terrorists poisoned the food supply?"

The survivalist squinted his eyes knowingly, as if he were in on some plot to which no other human being was privy. Adam didn't know what to say. He stared back for a moment then, stunned, walked away to catch up with his lumbering tour group.

Five minutes later Adam was leading the group along the duck pond. He looked up and saw a familiar sight.

"Oh, look, everyone," he said. "We have a duck in flight directly—"

Boom!

A loud gunshot rang out over the duck pond as Adam and the tour group hit the deck. The survivalist's rifle was still smoking as he ran past Adam to claim his prize—a dead duck floating in the water.

When Adam realized that the survivalist had killed one of his beloved birds, something deep inside him burned. Adam had spent months in this park, and he knew some of these birds intimately; by now he was acquainted with their particular quirks and idiosyncrasies. Adam could not stand up for himself in life, but he could stand up for others—especially animals.

Adam leaped to his feet and, with superhuman strength, sprinted to the survivalist and body-slammed him onto a patch of mud near the bank of the pond. The survivalist and

Adam struggled, rolling around as the tour group watched in horror. Some of them took pictures.

Just then, Steve came jogging across a small bridge above the pond. The sounds of the tour group members screaming for help and the grunts and epithets of Adam and the survivalist caught his attention. He dialing 911 just as Adam triumphantly grabbed the rifle, cocked the chamber, and held the defeated survivalist on the ground.

Moments later two police officers arrived. Steve watched them handcuff the duck killer and remove him from Adam's watch. Adam returned to his bird-watching tourists, who were holding each other and crying like baby seals that had barely escaped a bludgeoning.

"I am so sorry. This usually doesn't happen," a mud-caked Adam told them. But they didn't buy this. The incident had confirmed their deeply held beliefs about the violent nature of New York—even though the man who was responsible for their trauma made his home in a toolshed in Alabama, as the police later discovered.

"Long live the NRA!" the survivalist screamed as the boys in blue led him away.

Adam spun around, angry. His anger often took him by surprise, now that a lifetime of repressed rage was finally bubbling to the surface.

"Long live…NPR! Asshole!" he cried.

When Steve heard Adam shout, he perked up. He had heard that voice before. He had heard that sense of righteous indignation conveyed clumsily through sibilant *s*'s. He approached the muddy city employee.

"Hey, are you okay?" he asked. Adam was pressing on his chest and wincing.

"Uh, yeah, yeah, I just bruised a rib, I think," he said.

Steve stepped directly in front of Adam to get a good hard look at his face.

"Oh, my God!" he exclaimed. "It is you—the dog guy!"

Adam stopped his personal examination and took in Steve, who was wearing a tank top, fanny pack, running shorts, and not much else. Steve's muscled torso glistened with dewy sweat, and Adam was both excited to see him again and horrified for Steve to see him in this condition. Adam's ranger outfit was trashed and covered with drying mud, as was his face.

"Oh! Wow. Hi," he said. "I didn't recognize you out of your scrubs."

A beaming smile lit Steve's face. "I didn't recognize you either. How's your dog, speaking of bruised ribs?"

"He's all better. Pees on the floor sometimes. Or is that me? Ha ha ha ha."

Steve didn't laugh. Adam might as well have just stuck that muddy boot of his into his stupid mouth. He sighed and began walking. Remarkably, Steve followed.

"So, uh, you run a bird-watching tour here?" Steve asked.

"Yeah—and you thought you were the only one to deal with crazies."

They shared their first laugh. The afternoon sun bathed Steve in a golden light. Adam tried not to stare at him for fear of being transparent in his desire. Adam thought Steve was so beautiful, but he didn't want Steve to know it—not just yet.

"That was pretty heroic of you, tackling that guy, getting all *dirty*." Steve's sphincter tightened as he got a whiff of the mud covering Adam.

"Well," Adam replied. "It was heroic of you to save my dog, and I don't mind getting dirty."

"Oh, yeah, I know."

Adam stopped walking and decided to make an amends—something he was learning how to do in AA.

"Listen," he said. "I owe you an apology. I'm sorry I was such a mess in the hospital—"

But Steve interrupted him and pulled a handkerchief from his fanny pack.

"Wait, wait," he said. "Here, let me do something. Here, look at me."

Steve leaned into Adam until they stood almost nose to nose. Steve then gently touched Adam's muddy cheek with the handkerchief. Adam tried to stay still; he was enormously moved and turned on by this very intimate gesture. Steve slowly wiped the mud from Adam's face and looked deeply into Adam's eyes. For a brief moment, he had an almost over-powering sense of recognition, but he couldn't say why. Adam couldn't help but flash his big, toothy grin. When Adam smiled, his eyes twinkled and he exuded a strange mix of sen-suality and charm. Steve melted on the inside. Adam was a cute, warm person, and these qualities made Steve want to take care of Adam and stick his penis inside him all at the same time.

"There we are—much better," Steve said gently after he more or less cleaned Adam's handsome face. Adam recalled what Rhonda had said about going back to the hospital to see Dr. Hicks and the thousands of times she had encouraged him to be "more aggressive." Adam could be aggressive. He could tackle gun-toting criminals and run twenty city blocks in his underwear while he was carrying an injured animal. But he could not be aggressive with other guys. That was harder than anything. That took superhuman strength, which Adam did not possess. Nevertheless, he decided to "act as if."

"So, listen, I'm going to be an aggressive-type person here and ask you out to dinner sometime," Adam blurted.

Steve's reflexive aversion to accepting gratitude kicked in out of habit.

"Oh, no—you don't have to," he said.

"But I want to," Adam insisted.

"That's okay."

"I want to."

"You don't have to."

"I know, but I want to—"

"It's all right."

"I'd kinda like to—"

"That's fine."

"I know, but I'd like to—"

"It's okay, really—hey, I have an idea. Why don't I ask you out to dinner?"

Adam laughed nervously as the tables got turned.

"Nooo," he said. "That's okay."

"But I want to—" Steve insisted.

"You don't have to," Adam replied.

"I know, but I'd like to—"

"Well, I'm flattered, but—you know, I should take you out to dinner to thank you for what you did for Burt."

Steve looked down at his feet. Adam seemed so charming that it felt as if the earth were about to crash into the sun.

"Well, if it's just about your dog," he said, "you don't need to bother. But if you're asking me out on a date, like a romantic date–type thing, then I just might say yes to such an 'aggressive-type' person."

Adam smiled. "Well, actually, it just so happens to be a romantic date–type thing. So, yes, that's right."

They both laughed flirtatiously, and the crotches of their pants grew tight.

"Okay, well, how's tomorrow night?" Steve asked.

"Tomorrow night's great," Adam replied. "Where?"

"Um, how about right here in the park, say the bathhouse?"

Adam wondered if he had heard Steve wrong. "The boat-house?" he asked.

Steve was unfazed. They both ignored this Freudian glimpse into Steve's character—the kind of thing people often do at the beginning of a new relationship.

"How about Sona instead?" Steve suggested. "That restaurant on Sixth? At six?

"Okay, great," Adam said.

"Okay, great," Steve replied.

"All right, then, well, I'll see you there," Adam chirped as he waved goodbye. He touched Steve on his bare shoulder and walked away.

"See you then," Steve shouted out as he watched the muddy, messy, charming man walk away. Then he felt the cold mud on his shoulder and recoiled in horror.

Chapter Seven

The next day, Steve was walking on air. He had come home the night before and told a stone-faced Michael about the coincidence of running into Adam, the dog guy. Michael was not amused.

As Steve dressed for his date, he was at once nervous, excited, and conflicted. Michael was sitting on the couch he had lived on the last five years and eating pork ribs when Steve spun into the living area. He was dressed in gray slacks and a slate-gray button-down shirt. Steve looked in the foyer mirror and used his fingers to comb his soft blond curls.

"Are you sure you want to do this?" Michael wondered, his hands sticky with barbecue sauce.

"God, will you relax? You sound like a jealous wife," Steve cracked.

"Well, you'll have to change your whole lifestyle—he's got a dog. You'll have to hide all the knives."

Steve had always told Michael everything about the loonies who came into the ER and the hotties he banged at the gym. For the first time, he wished he had more boundaries with Michael. Michael knew him too well, and when people know you too well, they tend to resist any attempt you might make to break your own mold, even when break it you must.

"Michael, Jesus!" Steve exclaimed. "It's just a date. Besides, I'm thirty-six years old. Maybe I'm tired of one hot sexual encounter after another. Maybe I want to find out what it's like to have okay sex with the same person on a regular basis."

Michael choked on his pork. He couldn't believe what he was hearing. This was serious. He threw down his rib, stood up, and strode to the center of the loft.

"Well! I'm very disappointed in you, Steve," Michael said, his hands on his hips. "Obviously, you're not the person that I thought you were."

And like some grande dame, straight-guy Michael swept into Steve's bedroom area and dramatically stood behind one of the translucent dividers.

Steve stared at Michael's silhouette in amusement. "Michael, I can still see you," he said.

Adam had butterflies in his stomach as he approached Sona. He had never ever been on a date without the social lubricant of alcohol or pot to help him feel like someone worth dating. Tonight would be a first. He lad gone to an AA meeting beforehand and felt suitably secure to enter the high-end eating establishment in Chelsea.

Adam knew that Sona was a fancy restaurant. After he had agreed to join Steve there, he at first panicked. Adam made roughly $18,000 a year at his city job. He was poor, and when he did have extra cash, he spent it on Burt. Adam's Hell's Kitchen apartment was rent-controlled—an insane deal, which afforded him the opportunity to live in a city that for the most part seemed populated with wealthy kings. He budgeted thirty dollars for dinner—an astronomical sum for him. But he was so excited to go on a date with Steve that he didn't think twice. When Adam walked into the restaurant, he stuck out. Wearing an eye-popping, tight,

red muscle shirt and sassy bell-bottoms, he was the only
splash of color in an otherwise gray world. He spotted Steve
sitting at a table, waving.

As Adam moved toward Steve, the world seemed to slow
down. Steve stood up, smiled, and welcomed Adam in slow
motion. Steve was dressed so *expensively.* In his flaming-red
shirt, Adam felt like Bette Davis in *Jezebel.* But Steve didn't
even notice; he was smitten with Adam's down-to-earth sex
appeal.

After exactly eight minutes of intense flirtation between
the two of them, a waiter placed a Diet Coke in front of
Adam and an appletini before Steve. Steve glanced at Adam's
beverage as he sipped his own. "You don't drink?" he asked.

"Uh, no. I'm on antibiotics," Adam lied.

"Anything communicable?" Steve asked cheekily as vodka
warmed the back of his throat. Adam looked at him, confused.
It took him a minute to understand what Steve meant.

"Oh! No," he said. "No, nothing communicable. It's been
a while since I've communicated with anyone."

"Since you had sex?" Steve asked. "Like how long?"

Adam Bernstein was not skilled at withholding information. In fact, he had no filter whatsoever. Since he had no
booze in his system, he had the social skills of a retarded
Martian with Down syndrome.

"Oh, you know, not that long," he said with an affected
nonchalance. "Just like, oh, six months." Adam had not had
sex in six months because he had been sober for six months
(and ten days).

Steve gulped. The mere notion of no sexual activity for six
months was almost unbearable. "Wow," he exclaimed.

Adam saw he was losing Steve for the first time in the conversation. Not knowing what to do, he tried to recall any
recent encounter that could reestablish him as sexually viable
in Steve's eyes. "Well, I did hook up with this one guy on a
phone sex line. But he lied about what he looked like."

Steve nodded in familiar agreement. He knew this story and where it was going; he'd been there himself countless times.

Adam continued. "Yeah, when he showed up, he was, like, twenty years older and fifty pounds heavier than he said. And short—well, um, he was a dwarf, or a midget? I get them confused. Yeah, he had crossed eyes and burns all over his face—no ears. I think he might have been born with a hare-lip, but that could have been from the fire. Yeah. I don't think he should have lied about those things, ya know?"

Steve's jaw hit the table. "No" was all he could say. He wasn't sure whether Adam was being serious or making it all up. But in Steve's line of work, he was inclined to believe such outrageous things. Few things surprised him anymore.

"You know," Steve said, trying to change the subject, "I don't really go on dates. But when I saw you in the ER, you seemed—I don't know—you seemed familiar to me."

Adam was perplexed. "Hmm," he said. "Did you grow up on Long Island?"

"No, Texas," Steve replied.

Adam felt the conversation begin to flow again and got flirty. "You don't have an accent," he said.

Steve held his appletini and regarded it. "It comes back after a few of these. Where did you go to college?"

"I went to NYU briefly, but it didn't work out." It didn't work out because Adam had been too busy getting high to make it to class, but he didn't want to burden Steve with the ugly truth just yet. At the same time, Adam felt like he was lying to Steve by withholding information—and even Adam knew honesty was essential in a good relationship. Still, Adam was worried about honesty. Honesty didn't make him look so hot.

Steve looked at Adam's suntanned face and bright smile for a long time, then gave up. "I don't know," he said. "I guess it's just one of those things, huh?"

Adam grinned, then got an idea for a joke. "Well, I was in a porn movie once—maybe you saw it?" Adam arched his eyebrows seductively.

"Really?" Steve gulped. He was sure that was where he had seen Adam.

Adam smiled impishly. "No," he said.

Adam laughed loud and hard, amused at his own twisted sense of humor. Steve did not know what to make of this guy. He was a little weird, but to say Adam was entertaining was an understatement. Over the course of their dinner they both laughed easily and often. When the check came, Steve paid for Adam's meal too.

As Adam and Steve meandered uptown, they shared anecdotes about their jobs and general life philosophies about family, friends, and politics. Adam noticed that Steve often let Adam take center stage and kept plying him with questions, as one might expect from a psychiatrist. As they crossed the southern portion of Times Square, Adam was talking about his bird-watching tours.

"Well, business can be kind of slow in the winter, but it's a steady paycheck and I'm trying to 'keep it simple' right now."

Steve knew exactly what Adam was alluding to, but he humored him. "'Keep it simple?'" he asked.

Adam touched Steve's arm and stopped walking. Adam felt so safe with Steve, so comfortable.

"Steve, look," Adam said. "I don't have an infection. I'm in recovery. And part of *that* is being honest about *that.*

Steve knew this was coming. He smiled in a reassuring way. "Good for you, Adam," he said. "Good for you. Listen, I deal with a lot of people with addictive personalities."

"Yeah, well, my personality almost killed me," Adam replied.

Steve put on his therapist hat. He often did this to show off, and he was showing off to Adam. Being a therapist allowed Steve to seem like a caring person while also making him feel superior. "Was there some event that forced you to get sober?" he asked.

Adam began to get emotional—this was serious stuff. He took a breath.

"Um, yeah. I got really fucked up and—oh, this is hard…"

Steve held Adam's shoulders with both hands, a stabilizing gesture. "It's okay. It's okay."

Adam forged ahead. "Um, I slept with…a mime," he said.

Steve tried to suppress his puzzle reaction. "Like, um, a mime?" he asked.

Six months and eleven days earlier, Adam had gone on a four-day crystal meth binge. After barricading himself in his apartment with drugs and a stack of porn, his fourth day awake brought on a certain kind of paranoid delusion. Horny but with no partner to party with, he had gone online to look for sex. In his deluded state, he did a Google search for "big tops." Lo and behold, a listing revealed that the Big Top Circus was in town—in Queens. Out of his mind, Adam left his apartment and descended into the subway, grinding his teeth and pinching himself beneath his shorts. When he arrived at the Big Top, he wandered through the surreal low-rent carny and spied a fortyish-looking mime dressed in a body stocking, bow tie, and hat. The mime's face was covered in white face paint— just as Adam's had been when he was a goth. Something seemed right about this.

An hour later Adam's big top turned out to be a big bottom. Back at Adam's apartment, where Adam had lured the mime with the promise of more crystal, the two of them had the kind of sweaty, toxic sex you might expect in druggie encounters with circus personnel. As he was about to climax, the mime turned and faced a fucked-up Adam. The mime began to jerk and shiver as he masturbated his mime penis. He grabbed Adam's face when he was on the verge. Suddenly, the mime *mimed* a very intense orgasm—complete with silent scream. The mime's face took on a grotesque quality that was profoundly disturbing—so disturbing, in fact, that it forced Adam to snap out of his denial. He screamed. He knew in that moment that he was an addict and alcoholic of the most hopeless variety.

Steve could hardly imagine sweet Adam at the center of this horrific tale. Adam looked at Steve sheepishly, imagining this would be the moment when Steve ran away—through Times Square and back to the hospital where he would draw up paperwork to have Adam committed to Bellevue. Instead, something else happened. Something *wonderful* happened. Steve didn't run away. More than that, he seemed actually empathetic. He didn't think Adam was a freak for telling him "too much information" on their first date. He didn't judge Adam for being open and honest about his dark side. The miraculous thing was that Steve actually found Adam's openness attractive. He found Adam's openness brave. He was envious of the very honesty that embarrassed Adam.

They exchange a smile and continued to stroll up Seventh Avenue, the Great White Way warming them as the sun cooled.

"The next day I went to a meeting," Adam said. "I'd had all these plans—college, law school. Everything went down the toilet once I tried drugs. One day I woke up in my thirties with no education, no money, no friends—well, except for Rhonda. She's my best friend. Hey, if you want, we can go see her. She's a stand-up comedienne across the street at Lou's Laf Attax."

Steve was genuinely interested. "Oh, cool. I love stand-up."

Adam was genuinely shocked. "You do? Oh, well, okay. I really should stop by and support her. She's been having a hard time."

Steve was intrigued. "Having a hard time?"

Rhonda was bombing badly when Adam and Steve arrived. Her comedy act was becoming the 'shock and awe' of Times Square, drawing patrons who came to see just how truly awful she was. People couldn't believe that this formerly fat stand-up comic would still be doing fat jokes even though she was skinny. As Adam and Steve sat in the deserted club near the stage, Rhonda laughed at herself. As usual, she was the only one laughing.

"Hey, wake up! It's not over till the fat lady sings—and I ain't sung yet."

No one stirred. She was quickly becoming comedy road-kill. People slowed down and strained to see her dying onstage.

"Wow, tough crowd," Rhonda continued gamely. "Remember, ladies and gentlemen, if you throw any spoiled vegetables at me, I will simply eat them."

As Rhonda guffawed at her own jokes, Adam mustered the courage to peek at his date. To his surprise, Steve was grinning from ear to ear. *He may not be laughing,* Adam thought, *but grinning is definitely the best response Rhonda's gotten since she lost the weight last year.*

"Although pork ribs were my favorite," Rhonda said. "Feel free to throw those. Isn't it funny how the more ribs you eat, the less you can see of your own?" Rhonda did her "comedy face," which consisted of a certain cock of her head and a "Can ya believe it?" smirk.

When she mentioned ribs, Steve had another feeling of déjà vu. He studied Rhonda's face, then leaned into Adam.

"You know, I *know* her, I think," he whispered. Adam tried to recall if Rhonda had ever been to St. Luke's hospital. Both of them were drawing a blank. Suddenly, a loud cricket began to chirp somewhere in the back of the bar. At first Rhonda thought she might be imagining it the sound of crickets at that moment was too much of a cliché to be believed. Rhonda never thought such a thing might actually happen in real life.

Rhonda was stunned, but the show had to go on. "Are those chocolate-covered crickets I hear in the audience?" she said. "I ate a whole box of them once—talk about *Day of the*

Locust." Rhonda laughed hysterically, but no one else, not even her best friend, joined in.

After Rhonda's act Steve and Adam stood by the stage door, waiting for Rhonda.

"She was funny," Steve said.

"Oh, well, you're sweet to say that, but really she wasn't."

Rhonda emerged with a big, bulky bag slung over her shoulder and a brown More cigarette hanging from her mouth. She spied her best friend and smiled as much as a cigarette clinched between her teeth would allow.

"Aw, thanks for coming," she said. "What a shitty audience, right?"

Adam knew his friend was ill. He knew she was not ready to admit to herself that she was thin and no longer funny. But, like sleepwalkers, it would be dangerous to wake her. He nodded to the handsome man next to him.

"This is Steve," he said.

Rhonda turned and shook Steve's hand. "The doctor with the heart of gold. Very nice to meet you."

"Yeah, you too." Steve was struck even more forcefully by the impression that he'd met Rhonda before. "I—I know you, right?" he asked.

Rhonda stared at him. "Well, I was just onstage," she said.

Steve froze. He had figured it out. He remembered where he had seen her before. He almost couldn't believe it—he couldn't believe Rhonda was *that* girl.

"Yeah—Marie's. Marie's Crisis. You're the cocktail waitress at Marie's Crisis—that piano bar across the street from my apartment."

"Yeah, that's right. I work there too. This place doesn't really pay," she groaned.

"You don't recognize me?" Steve asked.

"No, honey. I'm too self-centered to notice other people."

Steve took the bait. "I'm sorry, did you say something?" he replied.

It took Rhonda a beat to catch up. Then she got Steve's joke and began laughing like crazy, which made Steve laugh too. For a moment, they laughed just as they had in the '80s. But they were so different now, almost unrecognizable to each other. When their laughter subsided, Steve excused himself to the restroom. Adam and Rhonda watched him walk back into the club.

"Oh, my God! He is so sweet and cute," Rhonda squealed.

"I know! He's so cute, and we've been having the best time. The more we talk, the more it's like I've known him my whole life."

"Past lives," Rhonda said sagely. Just then an old man slumping at a table near them came out of a booze-induced catnap. He noticed Rhonda standing near the exit.

"You're about as funny as a heart attack," he said.

"Aw, thanks, Dad," Rhonda replied.

After Steve returned and they said their goodbyes to Rhonda, Adam and Steve walked west and talked about their evening. It seemed that for all their differences on the surface, they were a lot alike on some essential level. They both had the same sense of humor. It was the first time either of them found that quality an aphrodisiac. As they approached Adam's building in Hell's Kitchen, Adam said, "Well, here I am." He gestured to the front door of his tenement. Steve made the move, reaching for Adam's hand. Adam pulled away and looked around worriedly. "What's wrong?" Steve asked.

"Well, aren't you worried about getting yelled at or gay-bashed?"

Steve laughed this off; it had never occurred to him to be afraid in New York. "No. Nothing like that has ever happened to me."

Adam nodded, but he was still wary. "It's just that every time I've expressed affection in public, some asshole from Jersey throws a beer bottle at me."

Steve arched his eyebrows. "Wow, sounds like you've had some pretty bad luck," he said.

Adam couldn't believe he was hearing this. It was as if Steve was psychic or something. Adam laughed nervously, not knowing how to respond.

"So, you wanna come up?" he said. "I'm sure Burt would be happy to lick you." Adam tasted his own shoe leather as he pulled his foot out of his mouth. But Steve was amused at Adam's complete lack of seduction skills. In a world of gay sex machines who devoured their partners like possessed, robotic porn stars, Adam's inability to play the part was a breath of air—fresh and warm and clean. Very clean.

As soon as Adam and Steve entered Adam's apartment, they knew they were going to have sex. It was just one of those things that had to happen. They just needed to have sex— that's all there was to it. Steve knew it; Adam knew it. Even Burt knew it.

After Steve petted Burt in the entryway, Adam attacked him with six months of pent-up need. They wrapped themselves around each other and kissed as if there were no other men in the world. Adam wanted to climb right inside Steve and live there for a long time. They fell onto the floor, making out and grinding their hard-ons into each other. Steve picked the smaller Adam up in his arms, strode to the bedroom, and threw him onto the bed, climbing on top. They ripped off each other's clothes—they couldn't be naked soon enough; they couldn't meld their bodies fast enough. They were impatient to be one.

As Steve dominated a willing Adam, Adam noticed that Steve was trembling in a way that made Adam think Steve was having an orgasm. Adam was disappointed. He had just gotten the man of his dreams in bed only to find the "doctor with the heart of gold" was also the doctor with premature ejaculation. Adam looked at him reassuringly.

"Did you come?" he asked.

The veins in Steve's face were bulging. If he was having an orgasm, it didn't seem to be subsiding.

"No. I think your dog is licking my foot," he grunted.

Adam bolted up to reprimand the other orally fixated Bernstein on the premises.

"Burt! Go to your bed!" he screeched.

Burt skittered away, like a character in a Bugs Bunny cartoon. Adam lay back on the bed. Steve was laughing. This was the oddest date ever, but somehow that made it the best. Adam apologized for the behavior of the dog that had brought them together a week before. "Sorry, I don't think he understands what's happening to his daddy." Adam groaned.

Steve perched up on one arm and lay next to Adam.

"Do you understand what's happening to his daddy?" he asked, looking intensely into Adam's eyes. Adam blushed.

"No," Adam said. But he did know. He knew very well, and in the spirit of honesty he changed his answer. "Yes."

Steve pulled Adam close. They kissed for a long time.

When the kiss ended, Steve said softly, "Hi."

"Hi," Adam replied.

Chapter Eight

Over the next month, Adam and Steve fell in love. They fell in love *hard*. They had sex and made love and talked and went to movies and had fancy dinners and wandered the streets of New York. They were in their own movie. It was the movie of their romance, and even if no one else was watching, they were. There were picnics and concerts in the park and lunches in Italian cafés.

All was going well until a particular dinner at a certain outdoor café. Adam, who had always been unlucky, became so caught up in his feelings of romance that he leaned over to Steve and kissed him in a very public display of affection. A man from New Jersey spotted this affront to nature and hurled an empty Rolling Rock beer bottle at the homosexuals. The bottle hit Adam smack-dab on the back of his head, and he went careening to the ground very ungracefully as Steve went to his aid. But gay love prevailed; aside from an annoying lump, Adam suffered no serious damage. He seemed used to such things, which intrigued a very confused Steve. Either Adam lived in a constant state of denial or the exact opposite was true—Adam lived in a state of blissful acceptance about his lot in life.

As their romance continued to ripen, Steve was simply astonished at the regularity of Adam's gay bashings. One little kiss seemed to make homophobes appear out of nowhere. It was like something supernatural. Eventually, Adam and Steve developed catlike reflexes to deal with the speeding bottles.

Throughout the month, despite all the bons mots and terms of endearment, there was actually very little real information exchanged about the past—about Steve's past, that is. Adam talked a lot about his sobriety and his embarrassing life choices, but Steve was very withholding about certain aspects of his past and personality. One afternoon outside Amy's Bread, a bakery on Ninth Avenue, Steve finally began to open up.

"You'll never believe this, but I wanted to be a dancer when I was younger," he said. "But it was such a messy lifestyle—very messy."

Adam pulled a cookie out of the bag of freshly baked goodies Steve had just purchased. Now that they were in a relationship, they rewarded themselves with the food of romance: carbs.

"When was your last relationship?" Adam asked.

Steve hesitated. "Um, by relationship, what exactly do you mean?"

Adam stared at him blankly. This was not a trick question.

"Your last boyfriend? Lover? Homosexual lifetime-commitment longtime-partner companion?"

Steve took Adam's cookie and bit off a morsel. "I've never really had one, I guess. No one's ever held my interest for that long, you know?"

Adam smiled. "Great."

Steve suddenly realized what a horrible thing this might be to hear from a man who is romancing you. He hastened to explain.

"Wait! No! I'm sorry, that sounds—listen, when I was a kid, I imagined I'd grow up, meet a nice guy, and have a big wedding. It would all have to be a certain way—I guess like in the movies I'd seen."

This struck a cord with Adam. "Me too," he said. "Yeah, I would always watch those movies and superimpose myself over the man, then the woman—like, I'd go back and forth. Like, in one scene I'd be Julia Roberts, and in the next scene I'd be, well, Julia Roberts."

Steve beamed. "Really?" he said. "I'm Meg Ryan."

Adam laughed and moved in to kiss the very witty and charming male Meg Ryan before him. For the first time, there were no beer bottles. They hugged and strolled down the street, eating their cookies.

"Hey, have you ever gone gay two-stepping? The Big Apple Rodeo in Chelsea?" Steve asked.

Adam looked at Steve in wide-eyed bafflement. "Two-stepping? No, I can barely one-step. What do you wear to something like that?"

Michael lay on the couch, doing something that he was very good at: nothing. He had been watching soft-core porn on one of New York's public-access cable channels. Michael mused that public access was the only place these days where he saw natural boobs instead of implants. As he pondered this, Steve sauntered into the living room dressed in complete cowboy regalia: boots, Wrangler jeans, ten-gallon hat—the works.

"Oh, look, it's Wyatt Earp," Michael exclaimed. "Should I call ya Wyatt, or do you prefer Mr. Earp?"

Steve dug through a catchall bowl, looking for his digital camera. Michael had misplaced it again after taking photos for his personal ad on a pornographic Web site.

"Might I remind you who pays the bills around here?" Steve moaned.

Michael resembled a frog with a slight beer belly. "You can tell me, but I might forget," he croaked.

Just then, Adam Bernstein, the gay Jew from Long Island, emerged from the bathroom dressed just like his cowboy companion for the evening. When Steve saw his date, he hooted and hollered, as if he were calling a pig.

"Yeeehaawww! Oh, my God, you look adorable." Steve laughed as he pinched Adam's ass through his heavily starched jeans. Adam could barely walk in this outfit. The jeans were so stiff, he moved as if he were playing Frankenstein on *Hee Haw.* Adam's boots were *not* made for walking.

"I feel like I have hooves," he said.

Steve let Michael know he should rise from his nest on the couch and take their picture. Michael rose begrudgingly.

"Oh, well, yeah, "Michael said. "I can't wait to take a picture of this. This is like Winger and Travolta together again—magic!" Steve put his arm around Adam, and Michael made the camera save this moment forever. Adam's eyes were closed. Michael grumbled on his way back to the couch. "You know, they'd never make that movie today."

Steve led Adam toward the door. Adam, who was trying to forge a relationship—any relationship—with Steve's best friend, stopped and regarded the slumping straight.

"Michael?" he asked. "You sure you don't want to come with us? Kick your heels up?"

Michael sat and went inside himself. He imagined the horrors a gay two-stepping night might entail—the men arm in arm with other men. He imagined these men all attacking him, trying to make love to him on a bale of hay as he cried and screamed. Eventually, after he had played his tape completely through, he turned to Adam and Steve, who were waiting for a response.

"No, that's okay. Thanks," he said.

With that, Adam and Steve were off. The country version of the shrink slapped the Western-garbed bird-watcher on the ass as they left.

Michael got up from the couch. He walked over to the

fridge and gazed into its empty interior. Discovering some ancient sorbet in the freezer, he peeled off the lid, scraped several inches of ice off the top, and went back to the couch to continue watching television.

Flipping through the channels, he landed on *The Oprah Winfrey Show.* A despondent woman sat across from Oprah and openly wept. Runny mascara streaked her scrunched-up face like squid ink. Michael raised the volume—he was highly concerned for this woman's well-being.

"How did you know your husband was cheating on you?" Oprah asked.

The woman mustered enough courage to form some semblance of a sentence.

"He started going to this honky-tonk near our house—this two-stepping place," she said.

Michael sat up. The woman continued.

"He said he was just going to dance, but I had a feeling there was this other woman in the picture. Of course, I just figured I was being needy or insecure."

"You didn't listen to what your inner voice was telling you?" Oprah asked.

The woman choked back sobs.

"No, I didn't, Oprah, but I knew I was losing him. I knew it."

Michael's eyes began to fill with tears as he found himself empathizing with this middle-aged housewife. He took a big bite of the chocolate sorbet that was freezing his crotch.

"What happened then?" Oprah asked gently.

"Well, he would get all gussied up, saying he was going to blow off some steam. It wasn't that I was jealous of his interest in dancing—I mean, we gave each other plenty of space to have our little adventures—but this woman had entered the picture right under my nose, and I lost him. While he was out falling in love, I was home, watching your show, getting fat on my favorite—chocolate sorbet."

The woman collapsed into Oprah's well-worn arms. Michael gagged on the frozen dessert sliding down the back of his throat.

He turned the channel back to porn.

There is something about living in New York City that immunizes most of its citizens of one of Adam's most familiar states of being: embarrassment. Adam was used to being embarrassed. He had grown up feeling embarrassed by his family, embarrassed by his inability to be "cool," embarrassed by his embarrassment. For some reason, hailing a cab while he was dressed like a cowboy embarrassed Adam a lot. But Steve's enthusiasm was infectious. Steve was exuberant, and Adam was under his Southern spell.

As they entered the lobby of a large prewar industrial building on Twenty-first Street, Adam was confused. This place seemed better suited for finance than for dance. Steve pushed the button for the elevator as they stood conspicuously alone in the marble and concrete foyer. Suddenly, the elevator doors opened, revealing two huge men dressed in ten-gallon hats, chaps, and boots. They sported handlebar mustaches and scowling expressions that looked a good foot or so above the diminutive Adam. The cowboys walked toward the street, their spurs scraping on the polished floor.

The lovebirds kissed and held hands as they rode the elevator to the eighth floor. The door opened and loud vintage Dolly Parton music greeted them. They stepped into a small lobby where they paid a cute gingham-clad hunk five dollars to get their hands stamped. Steve then led his date down a small hall.

Adam and Steve burst through the front door of the Big Apple Rodeo, which was taking place in a large, spacious loft. The space had no windows and no real character except for the decorative bales of hay in the corner and a few inflatable cactuses. Most of the patrons were Southerners who had moved to New York to escape gay persecution, only to find themselves waxing nostalgic for their lost culture once they were liberated.

As Adam took in the scene, his jaw dropped as he observed big queeny cowboys twirling each other around like—well, big queeny cowboys. Several cowgirls—both butches and femmes—also followed suit. Couples of all shapes and sizes swirled in a whirlwind of cheerfulness. "Oh, my God, it's a hoedown," Adam blurted. Steve laughed and led his little man through the gliding and twirling two-steppers until they reached a spot near the middle of the revelers where they could enter the "parade." Steve took Adam's hand and began to move when Adam interrupted him.

"I don't know how to do this," Adam yelled over the raucous country music.

"It's easy," Steve said. "Just relax. It goes 'quick, quick, slow; quick, quick, slow.' It's just a repetition of the same move, only we're gonna be goin' that way." Steve had suddenly rediscovered his Texas accent.

Adam decided that two-stepping must be like swimming: The only way to learn was to jump in feetfirst—or hooves-first, as in this case. Steve took the lead, placing one of Adam's hands on his shoulder and the other on his waist. To Adam, this two-stepping thing looked a lot like your basic ballroom dancing, although the last time he waltzed was at his own bar mitzvah. He had danced with a lot of people that night, mostly older female relatives, and none of them had resembled the strapping shiksa god standing before him. Steve's blond tresses curled from just beneath his hat, which would have made his face innocently angelic if he weren't so sexy.

Steve literally swept Adam off his feet. Steve was so strong, and he seemed taller in his boots. As Adam and he scooted along the shiny, buffed wooden floor, the rest of the world went away. Suddenly, the appeal of this couples-dancing thing began to dawn on Adam. He struggled with the steps, trying to do his best not to step on Steve's feet.

"Ow!" Steve yelled when Adam inevitably gave Steve's toes a good stomp.

"I am so sorry!" Adam cried.

Several of the other patrons of the Big Apple Rodeo noticed Steve nursing his injured foot while Adam stood beside him, mortified. Steve recovered and sidled back to his partner.

"It's okay. Let's try again," Steve said. Now Adam was terrified. In his boots lay devastating powers to kill and maim. He put his hand back on Steve's shoulder. They listened for the beat, and once they were hooked in, Steve began to lead Adam across the dance floor.

After they began moving again, Adam was extremely aware of his feet. He wasn't, however, conscious of his knees, one of which flew into the space between Steve's legs, turning his balls into ovaries.

"Oooooohh!" Steve squeaked as he bent over, the wind knocked out of him—and his balls.

"I'm sorry. Oh, my God, I am so sorry!" Adam shrieked.

Once Steve's testicles had returned to their normal and upright position, he took his date in his arms again. He was determined to keep going—to mold Adam into the person he wanted to be with. That person would know how to two-step.

"It's okay," Steve said reassuringly. "You're new to it. Let's try again."

Adam wanted to be the person Steve wanted him to be, so he tried his very best to be someone he wasn't—say, a cowboy. Aside from his bar mitzvah there had been few occasions when he had danced publicly while he was sober. There weren't many grown-up things he had done sober. Nevertheless, he caught the rhythm, and the two of them began to make some headway. Steve was duly encouraged.

"There you go," he said. "See, you got it."

Steve spun Adam around dramatically, which made Adam laugh as if he were on an amusement park ride—the Steve Hicks Tilt-a-Whirl. Just as he regained his footing, Adam realized that they were standing next to a towering wall of muscle wearing a plaid shirt with cutoff sleeves, a ten-gallon hat, and painted-on jeans. The rodeo stud was staring at Steve and slowly chewing gum with a knowing look on his face.

"Hey, Steve," he said with a leer.

Steve looked as if he'd been hit in the face with a frying pan loaded with Jimmy Dean sausage. He struggled to respond.

"Uh, hi, Andy. This is um—"

"Adam," Adam said.

Andy, who was blond and tan and had a hot corn-fed look that was the antithesis of Adam's Jewishness. Andy was porn-hot, but unlike most porn stars he was also tall: around six foot five in his boots. He regarded the awkward Adam's askew hat and pants that were pulled up too high.

"Looks like someone's having a little trouble here," he said patronizingly. Adam tried to save face by making a joke.

"Yeah, well," he said. "I'm Jewish, so give me a 'bottle dance' and I'm fine." Adam laughed desperately as Andy stared at him. Apparently, his reference to *Fiddler on the Roof* had fallen on deaf goy ears. Adam looked at Andy's mouth. He imagined Steve's penis in it. Then Adam imagined Andy cooking him in an oven and eating him for dinner with grits.

"Well, I teach private lessons here, if you ever want to take this seriously," Andy growled.

Steve piped in. "Yeah, Andy's a really good instructor."

Andy looked at Steve lasciviously.

"Not that you ever needed any instructing," Andy said, winking at Steve. "And your dancing wasn't bad either." Andy turned to Adam. "Shalom, Cowboy," he said.

With that, Andy launched into an impressive series of

backflips across the dance floor. The rest of the patrons seemed used to this sort of thing. Andy was the king of New York's Big Apple Rodeo. He was the steroidal love child of Roy Rogers and Dale Evans.

Awestruck at Andy's feat of Olympian superiority, Adam turned back to Steve. "Oh, my God. I'm terrible at this," he said.

Steve was determined to move beyond this uncomfortable moment. He took Adam's hand and began to catch up to the jaunty beat just as the music gently segued into a slower love song. Gays and lesbians of all shapes and sizes pulled their partners close. Adam smiled, and Steve smiled back.

Ah. See, this is better," Steve said. He held Adam close, their noses almost touching.

"This is just like any slow dance," Adam sighed.

"That's right—only in heels," Steve replied.

Adam laughed. He liked this relaxed and more comfortable side of Steve.

"I used to be a good dancer," Adam said.

"What happened?" Steve asked as he playfully wrinkled his nose.

"Have you ever been to a sober dance? I hate to point this out, but dancing is ninety percent beer. And a hundred percent cocaine."

When Steve heard the *c* word, he recoiled.

"Ugh. Cocaine is such an ugly drug," he said.

Adam looked at Steve. Never in a million years would he have guessed this composed, suave gentleman was also the coked-out Tasmanian Devil he had met in the '80s.

"Haven't you ever been addicted to anything?" Adam asked.

"No. Well, *Golden Girls* reruns," Steve confessed.

Adam gave him a teasing stern look.

"Wow," he said. "That one is harder to kick than heroin. How'd you do it?"

"I switched to *The Nanny,* then gradually tapered off."

"Um, I have to leave now," Adam quipped. "All this talk

about Lifetime Television for Women is triggering me. I don't think I can handle all this nice dancing."

Steve laughed. He overpowered his diminutive date and dipped him dramatically. "What about *dirty dancing*?" he snarled.

After Steve pulled a laughing Adam back up, Adam had to comment on Steve's new persona. "You're in a mood," he said. "You're like a different person tonight."

Steve grinned from ear to ear. "Well, I'm happy. I'm dating someone."

Adam looked back at Andy, who was doing head spins in the middle of the dance floor as a small crowd cheered him on. "That guy Andy is really hot," he remarked. Steve didn't take his eyes off Adam.

"I guess so," Steve said, "but he's not my boyfriend." He looked intensely into Adam's puppy-dog eyes. "You are."

Adam repressed a gasp. He had never heard those words before in his life. He looked at the handsome dreamboat who had been the first one to say it, then kissed him for a long time. They collapsed into a hug as they slowly moved to the love song. Somewhere in that sweaty Saturday-night crowd, two boys became boyfriends. Somewhere in the crowd, a gay Jewish cowboy finally felt safe in the arms of someone else.

Chapter Nine

Adam's sense of security was short-lived. It didn't take long for him to start worrying. A few days after Steve's proclamation, Adam began to remember that things just didn't usually work out for him in life. Why would this time be any different? Adam had a habit of killing hope before its roots got too deep. He always felt he had to prepare himself for inevitable disappointment. He met Rhonda one afternoon in Sheridan Square for a tête-à-tête.

Nestled in the West Village just steps away from the historic Stonewall Bar, Sheridan Square marked the location of the beginning of the gay rights movement in 1969. Shaped more like a triangle than a square, the small park contains several benches and a few scruffy shrubs, but its most distinctive features were its statues—life-size casts of two gay men with rather large bulges in their pants who seem to be negotiating something, like, say, where to have gay sex. A matching pair of lesbians on another bench seemed to negotiating something else, like, say, where to find cheap lumber.

Marie's Crisis, the piano bar that provided Rhonda with her second job, was within spitting distance of Sheridan Square on Grove Street. Rhonda and Adam would often meet in the park on her lunch break or when Adam was on his way to one of the many AA meetings that he frequented downtown.

Picking up a nonfat latte at Starbucks, Rhonda sauntered over to Sheridan Square to wait for Adam, who was running late. Rhonda sat next to the bronze lesbians and smoked a cigarette while she wondered what to do with her life. Her stand-up comedy job at Lou's Laf Attax was going nowhere. Her other job at Marie's didn't pay enough to keep her head above water—especially in Manhattan, which was fast becoming an island for the rich and not for struggling comediennes, skinny and fat alike.

Rhonda looked at all the gay history around her. She knew she walked a tightrope between two worlds. Lou's place was likely the most horrific bastion of straight male power, while Marie's was almost cartoonishly gay. Rhonda had always hated that term *fag hag* and found it very demeaning. It marginalized straight women who had gay friends and suggested they were needy and unable to open up to straight guys. All of this might be true of Rhonda, but for reasons having nothing to do with Adam. It seemed to her that since she was Adam's friend before he came out of the closet, she was exempt from any easy labels. Though the fact that she was one of two female cocktail waitresses at a historic gay piano bar in the Village made the label a little harder to dismiss.

Rhonda didn't relate to the so-called fag hags she saw on TV or in movies who treated their gay best friends as surrogate husbands. She loved Adam, but she didn't want to have sex with him. He *got* her—understood her in a way the monosyllabic straight guys she met just didn't. She saw him more as a girlfriend, and she didn't really have many friends, male or female. After she lost the weight, she became guarded and suspicious. While she was thrilled that Adam was dating this doctor, it was her job as his friend to watch his back, just in case.

Adam emerged from the Christopher Street station underneath the Village Cigars shop and crossed Seventh Avenue to meet his friend. Almost immediately, he launched into a much-needed therapy session with Rhonda, who knew him better than anyone. When he told her that Steve had told Adam they were boyfriends, Rhonda's ears pricked up.

"You're sure he said 'boyfriend'? He didn't say, 'Boy, do I need a friend'? she asked, sipping her coffee.

"Yeah," Adam said. "I didn't know what to say to him. I mean, sometimes I look at him when I'm in the moment, and I have these feelings—like I cherish him? But then I'm always waiting for the other shoe to drop like it always has."

Rhonda knew this side of Adam—the victim side. She gently nudged Adam through her opinions. Even though this dynamic had been in place for decades, Adam and she still almost always got defensive with each other. Their mutual defensiveness was part of the process. They would disagree at first, then eventually the other's assessment of the situation would take hold.

"Well, he seems to be moving awfully fast for a psychiatrist," Rhonda noted. "I mean, this whole romantic-myth stuff is a recipe for disaster. He's a shrink—he should know this."

Adam had expressed concern that Steve was rushing into this relationship. Then he felt mad at Rhonda for accusing his boyfriend of rushing into the relationship. He could criticize Steve, but what did she know?

"Well, yes, he is a shrink," Adam said. "But I think he knows more about this stuff than us. He has a degree. We just have Oprah.

Rhonda pondered this truism. "You know, Oprah has made it impossible for me to have a close relationship with anyone besides Oprah.

Adam finally admitted the thing that was at the heart of his doubts about his relationship. "I mean, he's so *normal*," he said, "and I'm such a freak. We're really different."

Rhonda knew what Adam meant. Being freakish was what they had in common.

"Well, I think that's good," she said. "The thing about you gay guys is that you're obsessed with finding carbon copies of yourselves. At least with guys and girls, we know we'll never figure one another out, so when stuff comes up we just say, 'Oh, he's just being a man,' or 'Oh, she's just on the rag.'"

Adam considered this. He had never thought about it, but Rhonda was right. He often saw this sort of gay narcissism all around him. For Adam, though, the idea of dating someone who looked and acted just as he did made his stomach turn. Perhaps there was something to be said about low self-esteem—he would never want to date himself. Maybe the differences between Steve and him were a good thing after all.

"Have you had a fight yet?" Rhonda asked.

Adam looked aghast, as if such a thing were unthinkable. "No!" he exclaimed. Then, growing insecure, he asked, "Is that weird?"

Rhonda sighed. "Well, you do have some things in common: He two-steps; you twelve-step."

Adam laughed. It amazed him that, offstage, Rhonda was one of the funniest people he'd ever met. He had attended her shows when she was obese and laughed until he was gasping for air. But ever since she lost the weight, she couldn't be skinny and comfortable as a performer—she felt too exposed. The second the spotlight hit her, she had to imagine she was fat again. But Adam knew she could overcome her fear and be as funny on the stage as she was off. Just as she was determined to help him understand his relationship, his mission was to help her realize her true talent and to pull her out of denial.

"You know, maybe your comedy is like my love life?" he said. "Maybe if you stop trying so hard, it will come."

Rhonda moaned. She hated to hear this, but she knew it was true. Still, she was predictably defensive.

"But fat jokes were my forte," she whined. "Being fat was the only funny thing that ever happened to me. It's the only thing some idiot on the street would find interesting about me."

Rhonda and Adam sat on the bench and gathered their thoughts. A homeless woman walked by and noticed that they were sitting in the same poses as the female statues, but they were completely absorbed in thought and totally unaware of this fact.

A few weeks later, Michael approached Rhonda, whom Steve had invited to his indoor Labor Day picnic.

"Hi, I'm Michael," he said. "So...Steve tells me you used to be fat?"

Rhonda stared at Michael as they stood at Steve's dining room table. Several upwardly mobile friends of Steve's flitted about, loading their plates with low-carb hot dog buns and gossiping about celebrities. Rhonda had quickly grown bored with the astonishingly shallow crowd. It wasn't helping that the only straight guy at the party was this little scalawag.

"Oh, really?" she said coolly. "Adam told me you used to be short."

Rhonda towered at least six inches above Michael. He was dressed in grungy shorts, and his beer belly and pale, hairless legs were obviously offending the other guests. Heedless of Rhonda's dismissal, Michael forged ahead.

"So, were you, like, fat or circus fat?" he asked.

Rhonda couldn't believe the gall of this evil troll.

"You know, you really ought to be standing when you insult a lady," she said. "Oh, wait, you already are."

Michael blinked at her—he honestly didn't get the jibe. So he continued. "What did you do with all that loose skin? Did you, like, donate it to a burn unit or something?"

Rhonda picked up a carrot—the only thing on the buffet she, a former circus fat lady, could eat.

"No, I gave it to the little people," she said. "The real little people, not the fake little people like you." With that, she bit down on the carrot and snapped it with her teeth. She imagined it was Michael's penis she was chomping as she walked away.

Steve had been planning his party for weeks. His huge loft space—with bountiful light streaming in through the wall of windows that faced Grove Street—was perfect for such a fete. He had sent out invitations to all his friends and hired the best caterers to whip up his favorite cuisine, Southern food. Steve had recently discovered a chef who was able to make all of his favorite dishes but without the fat or carbs.

After five months of dating, Steve felt ready to introduce Adam to his friends. Of course, Michael had already met Adam, but Michael had less stature than a retarded foster child Steve sponsored. Steve believed—wisely so—that until lovers accrue a sufficient amount of time alone together, a prospective mate should not be forced to meet his partner's friends. All these months Steve and Adam had been building a foundation of intimacy. If Steve had rushed Adam to jump through hoops in an attempt to impress his friends, he would have put too much pressure on the relationship.

Across the room from the buffet table, Adam helped Steve with the business of the party. Bowls where filled with fancy nuts and fat-free chips. Adam was reaching for a jar of twenty-dollar pickles when he saw a bright-orange plastic plate with matching bright-green utensils. He picked them up and inspected them curiously.

"Whom are these for?" he asked.

"My friends Jeff and Geoff are bringing their new foster child," Steve said hastily as he busied himself with the thing he loved most: details.

"Ah, kids. I think I saw some of those on TV once," Adam said drily.

Steve repressed a stunned reaction. Inside his mind a red flag went up. Actually, the flag was pink.

"You ever think of having kids someday?" he asked cautiously.

Adam made choking sounds. "Uh, no. I already have one— myself."

Steve decided to clean up. This conversation was getting a little messy, so he instinctively began to wipe down the kitchen counter even though it was clean.

"Well, I love children," he said sharply. "I can't imagine anyone not loving kids." Just as he reached to organize Adam's perpetually messy hair, the front door opened. He turned and saw Geoff and Jeff arrive with a bottle of wine and a seven-year-old Asian girl dressed in her "native" wear—a kimono with chopsticks in her hair. She resembled a baby geisha and was obviously uncomfortable in this getup since she was actually from the Bronx.

"Hello," Steve said warmly as he went to greet his friends, who were dressed in matching Abercrombie & Fitch outfits. Jeff was blond, and his hair was so perfectly coiffed that Adam thought he resembled a bleached Mexican televangelist. Geoff was casually chic in an Upper West Side sort of way, with his sweater wrapped strategically around his shoulders à la *Brideshead Revisited.*

Steve ushered the three guests into the main area of the loft where everyone was mingling and eating. Geoff had an announcement to make.

"Hello, everyone. This is Ling Ling, our new foster child."

Adam watched all the white, clean-cut gays turn politely and wave at the young girl. All of Steve's friends looked the same. Adam recalled Rhonda's theory about gay narcissism—Steve's friends seemed to prove her right. The men in each couple looked more like brothers than lovers; Steve and he appeared to be the exception. Steve looked blonder and fairer next to Adam's dark hair and ruddy skin. He looked taller next to Adam's five-foot-eight 145-pound frame.

Now joining the party were two gays who not only looked alike but also had the same name—Jeff and Geoff. Steve moved this bluest of Blue States families toward the dining table, which was resplendent with food.

"Hey, Ling Ling, are you hungry?" Steve asked loudly. "We have hamburgers, corn—"

Steve talked to her like a child, which she was—but only on the outside. The spirit inside Ling Ling was not that of a child but of a being as old as Beelzebub himself.

"Suck the corn outta my ass!" Ling Ling screamed. The room fell silent. Adam couldn't believe his ears. He inched toward the other end of the table to get a better view of this tiny Asian devil.

Steve, not knowing how to respond, opted to deny the ugliness of the situation.

"Oh, my God. She's adorable," he crowed.

Jeff and Geoff also seemed to be gold medal–winners in the Denial Olympics. They joined Steve in his coddling of the wee terror. Deep inside this couple were two very good boys who had grown up to prove to the world that they weren't just cocksuckers but also bighearted gay saints who wanted to contribute to society in a positive way.

Jeff reached for a bowl of treats and presented it to his new daughter.

"Look, sweetie, dried fruit," he chirped.

Ling Ling looked at him and contorted her face as if she smelled something foul.

"Dried fuck!" she screamed.

Jeff pulled the offending fruit away, and all eyes were on them. Jeff's cheerful demeanor was beginning to crack and there was a slight tremor in his hands.

Jeff's lover, Geoff, put on his best Waltons persona. He bent down to face the tiny terror. "Now, Ling Ling," he cooed, "that's not nice. Tell Da-Da and Doe-Doe you're sorry."

The little potty mouth stood before them defiantly with her hands on her hips.

"I am not some little Hello Kitty doll to be paraded in front of every goddamn queen in town," she barked.

Jeff chuckled nervously. He turned to Adam and Steve.

"We just took Ling Ling to brunch in Chelsea," he said. "She was quite the hit."

A horrified Adam gently moved toward the tiny potty mouth. He stretched out his arms and offered her the orange plastic plate and green fork as a token of goodwill—an orange and green white flag from a white fag. But Ling Ling wasn't interested. She smacked the place setting out of Adam's trembling hands, sending them skittering across the floor as nelly queens screamed and scampered out of the way.

Steve needed to move the party along. He turned to the dads.

"So, who would like a drink?" he asked.

"I would," Adam said sarcastically.

Several hours later, Rhonda was becoming the Susan Sontag of this gay Labor Day party; she was frustrated by all the chatty mediocrity she was hearing. She decided it was time to read her *New Yorker* and thus shield herself with the protective armor of intelligence. She planted herself on an overstuffed chair by the wall of windows and checked out of the dumb gay party. Her highbrow magazine became a kind of anti-guppie Kryptonite.

By this point in the get-together, the partygoers had accepted Ling Ling's antics as simply part of the festivities. Adam had tried his best to tolerate the child—the progeny of crack-addicted parents, Steve had told him during a stolen moment. Adam was shocked. After trying to get his head around the fact that somewhere in the Bronx lived a crack-smoking Asian-American couple, he wondered if he had ever run into Ling Ling's birth parents at any meetings. It seemed there were never any Asians in his recovery meetings. He wished he were Asian; maybe he would have been smarter about his life.

When Adam went to Steve's pantry to fetch coffee, he found Ling Ling sitting happily on the floor, eating the very coffee grounds he was aiming to use for the guests. She sat there, brown granules around her little mouth, heading toward what had to be borderline caffeine poisoning.

"What are you doing? Stop that!" Adam exclaimed.

Ling Ling's eyes were bugged out. She growled at Adam, then dropped the coffee can and laughed maniacally. Adam bent over to pick up the can, and the runty monster slapped his face with the full force of her tiny hand. Then she screamed and ran back into the party.

Adam wanted to take the chopsticks out of Ling Ling's hair and stab her with them. He tried to feel compassion for this little one as his face stung and a red mark formed where she had struck him. She was after all a child, and a proclivity for using stimulants, whether crack or caffeine, was her biological parents' disease.

On the other side of the loft, just as Rhonda was becoming absorbed in an article about—ironically enough—the life of Susan Sontag, a speeding Ling Ling ran up and tried to pull the magazine from her hands. Rhonda resisted, and a fight ensued between a seven-year-old and a woman thirty years her senior.

"Stop it! Stop it!" Rhonda bitched. "Beat it!"

The goody-two-shoes gays that populated the apartment turned and looked at Rhonda disapprovingly for not simply giving her magazine to poor little Ling Ling. They all thought the same thing about her: *baby hater.* That the one person in the room who could actually give birth to a child was the one wrestling *with* a child didn't matter. Everyone watched Rhonda and Ling Ling in this tug-of-war, then looked at Adam, who had come to see what the fuss was all about, as if he were somehow responsible. Rhonda was Adam's guest after all.

Rhonda put her foot on the child's chest to get more leverage, leaving a large black shoe mark on Ling Ling's already frayed geisha getup. Finally, Rhonda yanked the magazine out of the clutch of the brat, sending Ling Ling flying into the sectional that bisected the living room. Ling Ling growled like a wild animal and sat arms folded on the couch next to her amused gay fathers who were still swimming up that river in Egypt. Adam sat next to Steve uncomfortably as the evil devil child hovered nearby like a rabid creature of the night.

"Girls will be girls," Steve chuckled knowingly. Adam was starting to have elaborate fantasies of breaking up with Steve, based on Steve's behavior at the party. His cool boyfriend had turned into a Stepford gay in the presence of his white, superior, perfect friends.

"Thank God we were able to pass the review for foster care. But, boy, did they put us through the ringer," Jeff said as he sipped his mojito, pinkie up.

"No one wanted our little angel," Geoff chimed in. "But that's why God invented gays—to care for all the unwanted children."

Adam held his coffee cup tightly. He imagined crushing it with his bare hands in frustration over this kid thing.

"That is so beautiful, Geoff," Steve said, tears filling his eyes.

Adam looked at Steve in disgust. He stood up dramatically.

"I'm sorry, but would you excuse me?" he said

He stalked away, chuckling contemptuously under his breath.

The party continued for several more excruciating hours until people gradually began to leave. Adam tried his best to converse with the guests, but he found he had very little in common with them. Steve's friends made Adam feel unbearably edgy and out of place, like Nancy Spungen at a cotillion. They all seemed oddly competitive with each other, as if there were an unspoken tournament to see who could be the most easygoing, least complicated, most precious gay in the world. As annoyed as he was with the mentality, Adam knew this was meant to be an opportunity for Steve's friends to meet him. He wanted to impress them for Steve's sake, but deep down he felt he hadn't made a very good impression.

After the sun set, only a few guests remained. Geoff and Jeff sat on the couch. Both of them were politely drunk by this point and still trying to restrain rambunctious Ling Ling.

Adam sat on a stool at the edge of the living room with a sour expression on his face. His terrible time was about to be made worse by the presence of Michael, who sat down next to him. Michael observed the bad seed squirming on the sofa and her gay dads, who were trying to keep her in check without spilling any precious drops of their cosmo cocktails.

Michael turned to Adam, grinning sarcastically. "Wow. Cute kid, huh?" he said. "Wonder if she's gay?"

There were times when Michael believed the whole world might be homosexual.

Adam frowned. "Well, your roommate is thinking about adopting one," he said.

Michael repressed a gag. He knew on some level that he was not only Steve's stand-in boyfriend but also his interim child. Now that Adam was in the picture, he only fulfilled one of those needs. Michael knew it was just a matter of time until Adam moved in and Steve asked him to move out, which of course meant the prospect of homelessness. This simply could not happen. Michael might have been the kind of guy who would fuck a horny homeless chick, but he had no intention of becoming homeless himself. So he decided to take a new approach—a stealthier one. He turned to his roommate's boyfriend and set his plan in motion.

"Look, I just wanted to say that I think it's cool that you and Steve are hanging out and doing your gay love thing."

Adam smiled. He had no idea a side such as this existed in the troll-like body of this gassy straight guy. "Aw. Thanks, Michael. That's sweet."

On the inside Michael cringed. His stomach turned. A gay man had called him "sweet." He braced himself and forged ahead.

"You know," he said, "before he met you, Steve was such a whore."

Adam's face dropped. Michael took no noticed and continued.

"Actually, no, that's not right. Whores get paid. He was just a slut. He would go the gym and hook up with, like, *hundreds* of guys every night—the hottest guys in New York just for the taking. I used to think of him as a sort of gay Hugh Hefner, ya know? And if I could be more honest with you?"

Adam looked at him blankly. *More honest?*

"Yeah," Michael continued, "I could never understand why he would give up on all that easy lovemaking, but I know you all want equal rights."

Michael had dropped his bomb, and judging from the look on Adam's face he had succeeded in his mission.

Adam sat on the stool, looking as if he had been punched in the stomach. He recalled Steve's interaction with Andy at the Big Apple Rodeo, but he didn't realize that was just the tip of the iceberg. Adam was hardly one to throw stones—his own history was filled with mimes and midgets and drugs and porn—but at least he had explained his past to Steve. It was called getting to know each other. Suddenly, Adam realized that all this time, Steve had sat quietly like a good shrink while listening to Adam expose his deepest, darkest secrets—but Steve had rarely reciprocated. He had never said, "Oh, yeah, I have a checkered past too." After feeling inadequate in Steve's circle of perfect friends, Adam realized that maybe Steve wasn't so normal or perfect after all. He had a past just as Adam had one. Adam sighed, and Michael spied Rhonda sitting across the room, her nose still deep in her *New Yorker*.

"Your best friend's cute," Michael said. "She's kind of a bitch though, right?"

Adam looked at his best friend sitting across the room. Rhonda looked lost in thought. He was too tired and too overwhelmed to lie.

"Yeah," he said.

After all the guests had left, Adam fumed as he watched his anal-retentive lover clean up the kitchen, which was a shambles. Sticky plates, wadded-up napkins, and half-eaten corn on the cob covered every available surface. Adam sat on the marble countertop that divided the kitchen from the dining and living area. Holding Ling Ling's plastic plate and utensils, he ceremoniously picked a wiener off the plate and, in an intentionally castrating move, bit the tip off when Steve glanced over at him. Steve barely noticed. He was mad at the dirt. Adam was mad at Steve.

"Children have replaced cock rings as the latest gay accessory," Adam said drolly.

Steve bristled. He hated this side of Adam—this holier-than-thou thing.

"Ling Ling is hardly an accessory, Adam. Why are you trying to pick a fight with me anyway?"

Adam slammed down the plastic plate and jumped off the counter, bracing himself for a fight. Adam knew he had a problem with anger. Even when he knew he was wrong, he just couldn't stop himself from saying how he felt.

"I'm mad because you project this image of the perfect boyfriend, and then Michael tells me—"

Steve jumped on Adam's words.

"What? *What!?*" Steve said. "He told you I was some kind of a whore, didn't he?"

"No!" Adam yelled. " 'Whores get paid.' He told me you were just a slut." Steve's hands began to shake inside the yellow

Playtex gloves he wore when he cleaned. He stormed around the kitchen, noisily rearranging the piles of party flotsam.

Adam pressed on. "It's okay. I would love it if you were a slut. I'd welcome any dark side at this point."

Steve passed Adam and began to clear items off the dining table. He held the debris precariously, as if he wasn't quite sure what to do with anything anymore. He had worried that Michael would open his big mouth. He had seen Adam and Michael talking, but for some crazy reason he thought Adam needn't ever know about his less than sterling reputation. He knew, however, that the best thing to do now would be to come clean about his past.

"Adam, okay, I admit I did play the field," he said.

"Sounds like you plowed the field," Adam snorted.

"I've been completely faithful to you, if that's what you're worried about," Steve muttered as he moved to the refrigerator.

"Of course you have," Adam said sarcastically. "You're playing the part of the perfect boyfriend—just like your friends. But I'm sitting here wondering, *Where is that slutty sex pig?* He's going to come roaring out again someday, and I'll feel like a fool for not having paid attention to the warning signs."

Steve began throwing things into a large garbage bag. He used his foot to press the refuse farther down into the bag.

"Oh, Adam, for Christ's sake!" Steve shouted. "Not everyone on this planet is intent on hurting or abandoning you."

Adam recalled his conversation with Rhonda in Sheridan Square and said, "People don't change just because they meet someone. That is so, like, Oprah 101. It's like I don't even know you sometimes."

Steve stopped and looked at Adam in disbelief. "What?" he said.

"I don't," Adam continued. "Who are you, Steve? You're a cowboy, a father, a slut, a shrink—which one is it?"

"My past is none of your business!" Steve yelled as he gathered empty beer bottles strewn next to the garbage can.

Beads of sweat were forming on his upper lip. He knew he was cornered.

"Oh, your past?" Adam said. "I didn't know you had a past—I've never heard about it. I've told you all of my horror stories. Where are yours?"

Steve spun around furiously. "Look, you have no right— *no right*—to qualify where I've been or what you think my 'dark side' is. I am not that person anymore. I am not that fucking person!"

Steve threw a beer bottle across the kitchen just as Michael peeped around the corner to watch the spat. "What's going—ugh," Michael grunted. The beer bottle landed smack-dab in the middle of his forehead and sent him careening backward. Neither Adam nor Steve moved to help him— it was his fault they were fighting in the first place. Adam sighed, hopped off the counter, and pulled Steve close to him.

"I'm so sorry," Adam said.

"Me too."

They hugged, knowing they had survived their first fight. That in itself took away some of the sting of the argument. They both knew that couples fight—they were now officially a couple.

Chapter Ten

A week later, Adam and Steve were perusing the bountiful produce of Dean & Deluca in preparation for their first Thanksgiving together. As Adam watched Steve look for the perfect turkey, he thought of all the previous turkey days he had been too stoned to experience. For working people who happen to be addicts, long holiday weekends do not provide the cozy warmth they afford most human beings. For addicts, holiday weekends are simply a four-day binge waiting to happen. But not this November: Adam was sober, he had a new boyfriend, and he was about to meet his boyfriend's parents, who were coming from some mysterious place called Texas.

The lovers walked through Greenwich Village to Steve's apartment. The fall leaves had transformed Grove Street into a rust-colored carpet. Adam was both excited and nervous about meeting Steve's folks. All Adam knew about them was that they lived in a mobile home and that Steve's father was a Baptist minister.

"What time do your folks get here?" Adam asked as he toted several heavy bags of food.

"They should be here in about an hour," Steve replied.

Adam knew it would be one thing to meet their son's gay lover. Meeting the Neanderthal who lived on the couch might be altogether too much.

"Did you put away Michael's porn?"

"Yes," Steve replied.

"Did you put away Michael?" Adam asked after a beat.

"He's at a Three Stooges convention at the Jacob Javits Center," Steve said drily. Adam took a moment to absorb this information: *They have Three Stooges conventions on Thanksgiving?* That seemed even more depraved than a holiday lost to drugs.

"Oh, I hope they like me," Adam said nervously.

It made Steve smile that Adam cared so much. "They should be worried about what you think," he said. "They're entering our world."

"Well, when you're a born-again Christian, your world follows you," Adam observed.

Steve stopped walking and turned to Adam to make his point. "They're not that religious anymore," he said. "Look, honey, I've been out to them for ten years. They've had plenty of time to get used to the fact that eventually I'd meet someone."

Adam smiled, and they walked the last couple of blocks to Steve's apartment building. Across the street near the entrance to Marie's Crisis, a redheaded man in a sleeveless shirt was unloading his belongings from a moving van. He watched Adam and Steve for a moment. When Adam leaned in to kiss his boyfriend warmly, the man hollered. "Ewwww! Fags!"

Adam broke from the kiss to espy the homophobe who had hurled such a hateful epithet. Righteous indignation welled up inside him. It was the same reservoir of pent-up anger that had enabled Adam to tackle a rifle-wielding survivalist. He stepped to the curb and yelled back, "Welcome to the West Village, asshole! Better get used to seeing fags!"

With that, Adam crouched into a ball, expecting the usual beer-bottle barrage. But no such affront came. The homophobe just stared in disbelief at his two fruity neighbors. Steve dragged his crouching boyfriend into the front door as the homophobe again yelled "Queers!"

A few hours later Adam sat at Steve's expensive dining room table, facing Dottie and Joe. Dottie was in her late fifties and exuded a warmth that was not dissimilar from Adam's. Beneath her shoulder-length blond hair, she wore a loose-fitting blue denim shirt with calico elbow patches. Joe was the male version of Dottie. They looked more like brother and sister than husband and wife: couple-twins, like Steve's friends. Joe was bald and every bit as handsome as his son. He seemed very uncomfortable, and Adam got the impression that Dottie had worked hard to convince her husband to take this trip to New York.

Joe took a nutcracker and opened a walnut loudly as Dottie did her best to fill the uncomfortable silence.

"You know, Jesus was a Jew," she said sweetly to her son's homosexual sex partner.

"That's right, he sure was," Joe chimed in, chunks of walnut in his teeth.

Adam was stunned but knew he had to respond.

"Yes, that's right," he said. "Sort of…ironic, isn't it, Mr. and Mrs. Hicks?" Adam tried to ignore another obvious irony. Mr. and Mrs. Hicks *were* hicks.

"Well," Joe continued, "I just can't get over how much New York has changed since I was here in '55."

Fishing for something to say, Adam remarked, "Well, if New York is about anything historically, it's change." It occurred to Adam that Joe didn't much like change. Perhaps he shouldn't have pointed out this fact.

Dottie seemed wistful. When she spoke, her tone was slightly ominous. "Well, I for one want to see Ground Zero.

Everyone back home wants an authentic Ground Zero T-shirt."

Steve caught bits of this conversation in the kitchen. Since he was presenting Adam to his folks, he thought he should just let them get to know each other. He was confident that Adam's sweet charm would win them over.

After topping off his scotch, Steve continued with the preparations for their Thanksgiving dinner. After donning a germ-protecting latex glove, he gingerly stuffed the turkey with gingerbread dressing. Every bit the Martha Stewart pro-tégé, Steve had saved clippings from Martha's magazines over the years for inspiration on just such an occasion. He opened one of his beech kitchen cabinets and removed an excellent bottle of merlot, which he set on the Italian-marble counter-top.

"Would anyone like some wine?" he called. He said it in a way that was very hoity-toity, as if he were a character in a Merchant-Ivory film. Observing the simpletons who had raised Steve, Adam realized just how far Steve had gone to reinvent himself. He couldn't believe that these people were Steve's parents. It just didn't seem possible.

Dottie played along, trying to be "fancy" like her son. "Oh, that would be *delightful*," she crowed.

Joe motioned to the kitchen with his nutcracker.

"Hey, open that box of zinfandel we brought," he suggested.

Steve's face dropped. He opened the refrigerator and stared at the box of wine his father had brought all the way from Texas. Steve looked for a corkscrew in the catchall draw-er, digging through ancient delivery menus from restaurants that had surely gone out of business. He found the corkscrew and retrieved the cardboard box that contained the sticky sweet booze that was his father's spirit of choice. Then it occurred to Steve that he had no idea how to open the box. There was no cork.

Adam sat at the table and stared at the Hickses. In his mind, he wrestled with possible conversation starters. He could think of nothing to say and was about to reach for the nut dish when Joe remembered something.

"Oh! Show Adam what we bought at the airport," he said to Dottie.

A look of awe swept across Dottie's sweet face as if in her purse lay the Arc of the Covenant. She reached into her bag and reverently removed the prize: the 9/11 commemorative plate Adam had seen on TV the day he stabbed Burt. Adam's face froze into a fake smile.

"Now, it's not for dinner," she explained. "It's just for decoration. It's made from *actual* ceramic chips from the site."

Steve came to the table, bearing two glasses of wine for his parents. After he served Joe and Dottie, he set down a steaming coffee mug in front of Adam. Dottie took a sip of her wine, then noticed Adam's cup.

"Well, don't you want some wine?" she asked.

Without thinking, Adam blurted, "Oh, no. I'm an alcoholic." When he realized what he had just said, he gasped for air, trying to suck this admission back in. Steve interceded to save the day.

"He's in recovery," he explained.

Dottie and Joe looked at Adam with a mixture of sadness and confusion, as if he had just told them he had cancer of the face. They clinked their wineglasses together, then took big gulps of the cheap boxed wine. They were getting *very* thirsty. Adam sipped his coffee. Suddenly, he remembered something his lover had told him about his parents.

"So, Steve told me that your anniversary is coming up soon?" Adam asked.

Dottie and Joe looked at each other affectionately. "Yep, forty years," Joe barked, as the wine warmed his insides.

"It feels like he proposed just yesterday," Dottie said, waxing nostalgic. Adam was touched, as many gays are when they ask straight married people about the sacred institution gay people are not allowed to have. "I suppose I said yes because I felt sorry for him," Dottie continued. "He was such a mess—had a drinking problem of his own back then. But I worked on him, got him to settle down, have kids. All men need women to tame them."

Dottie regarded Adam and saluted to him with her wineglass. "Someday, when you meet a nice girl, you'll know what I mean."

Adam stared at her, his eyes blinking receptacles of pure bewilderment. Annoyed, Steve strode in from the kitchen and dropped a plate of crudités atop his mother's 9/11 plate. He returned to kitchen, gulped his scotch, and picked up a rather large butcher knife. He thought about it, then went back to preparing his fennel and walnut salad.

As the evening progressed, Adam found himself in desperate need of a powwow with his boyfriend. Slipping into the kitchen area where Steve was cooking, he motioned for them to meet in the bedroom—although he worried that taking his lover to the bedroom in front of the Hickses might be a bad idea.

Once they were behind the folding screens that provided a modicum of privacy, Adam whispered in hushed tones, "I feel like I have a sign around my neck that reads 'I eat your son's ass.'"

Steve winced. "Oh, please," he whispered back. "That wouldn't even occur to them. Just behave the way you normally do. They're in New York now, not Texas."

Adam nodded his head furiously, as if he were getting a pep talk from an army general. Fortified with courage, he braced himself as they returned to the living room, where Dottie and Joe were standing in front of the wall of windows that faced Grove Street. The windows ran the length of the entire loft, facing the building across the street and affording anyone who cared to look a bird's-eye view of the goings-on in Steve's home. Before Adam, neither Steve nor Michael ever had sex at home—opting instead for shower stalls and homeless women-so it had never occurred to Steve that he needed to worry about his privacy.

When they returned to the living room, Adam was smiling, as if he were having a good time—which was far from the truth. Steve's parents seemed to be in the throes of the kind of über-denial of reality. Steve stood next to Adam and faced his parents with a strange look of determination on his face.

"Mom, Dad," he began, "I just wanted to say that normally Adam and I are very affectionate with each other, and we don't feel like it would be fair to us—or really to you—if we behaved in a way that somehow communicated that we are in any way ashamed of our feelings for each other. I think it's healthy that we express normal, healthy affection in your presence and, well, I just wanted to say that."

Everyone stared at each other a moment.

Finally, Dottie responded, as if she were just waking up from a long afternoon nap. "Oh, well," she said. "Don't not be y'all's usual selves just 'cause we're here." She laughed a laugh that was not actually a laugh but more of an amused whimper.

Joe's face was frozen. He could have been on Mount Rushmore. Finally, the stony façade crumbled. "That's right. Uh, we're all grown-ups here."

With that, the path was clear for Steve to make his move. In a dramatic gesture he lowered his left hand and opened his palm. The intention was clear—he would hold his boyfriend's hand in an act of "healthy, natural affection." Adam, who wanted to do the right thing, looked at Dottie and Joe, then at Steve. He took Steve's hand. They stood there together—out, proud gay men holding hands in the face of adversity.

Everyone heaved a sigh of relief, which was quickly interrupted by something awful. "Ew! Fags!" cried the familiar voice from across the street.

Everyone was shocked. Adam looked over Dottie's head

through the windows and saw that the homophobe he had yelled at earlier on the street had indeed moved into the apartment opposite Steve's. The odious man stood on his fire escape with a beer in his hand and leered at them all.

Dottie tried to make polite conversation as if none of this was happening. "So, where would a person find curtains for windows so big, son?" she asked.

Steve tried to lead his parents away from the windows and over to the kitchen area, but it was no use. They were in plain sight no matter where they went.

"Queers!" the drunk middle-aged man hollered.

Steve struggled to ignore the man, which Adam didn't quite understand. He suddenly saw Steve's parents' denial and need for propriety reflected in Steve. Adam wanted to open a window and throw a Molotov cocktail across the street. He couldn't understand why everyone else was acting as if this affront to decency weren't going on.

"Well, actually, there's this place downtown that I've been meaning to check out," Steve said. "But I think blinds would actually be more tasteful—"

"Cornholers!" the homophobe yelled.

Dottie and Joe moved to the dining room table, where they could sit and—more importantly—drink wine. Adam turned to Steve and whispered, "Honey, I don't think we should be expressing 'healthy affection' right now."

"Look, I told them we aren't ashamed. Just ignore it," Steve hissed.

Adam and Steve approached the shaken Texans. Dottie and Joe were looking forlornly at their freshly emptied wineglasses.

"How's that wine?" Joe asked. "Any left?"

Adam tried to be helpful. "Um, well, you drank it all," he said. "We don't have any boxes of wine, I can open an actual bottle."

"COCKSUCKERS!"

Dottie tried to ignore the homophobe's latest outburst. As Adam retrieved a bottle of wine from the kitchen, she said, "The *cock*screw is on the counter."

Upon realizing her Freudian slip she gasped and corrected herself loudly. "*Cork*screw, I mean."

"Got it—right here," Adam said. He grabbed the wine, something he could not let himself drink, and began screwing the curled metal into the cork. From the dining room, Joe watched Adam performing this task as Steve tended to basting the turkey behind him. Joe wasn't sure if it was the wine or just the influence of the man yelling from across the street, but for a split second it looked to him as if his son were sticking the turkey baster into his Jewish lover's ass. Joe blinked his eyes, ashamed at himself for imagining such a thing. He couldn't wait to go home and back to his recliner, where such horrors where safely hidden from view.

Flustered, Adam put the bottle of wine between his legs and pulled out the cork. It made a large pop that reverberated across the exposed brick walls of Steve's Spartan abode.

Adam moved toward the dining room table followed by Steve, who was hefting a delicious-looking turkey. Mr. and Mrs. Hicks gladly extended their glasses, which Adam filled with the dry wine. Then Steve and he sat down across from the other couple.

"Happy Thanksgiving," Adam said tepidly.

Dottie was swilling her alcohol when suddenly she remembered something else that was in her big Texan purse. She was quite intoxicated at this point, and her words slurred a bit.

"Oh, I forgot!" she exclaimed. Adam thought he heard a hiccup as she reached down and produced a medium-size Tupperware container from her bag. She removed its lid and showed its contents to Steve.

"Look, honey, your favorite. Mama's homemade—"

"Fudge packers!" the homophobe bellowed.

Dottie set the container of chocolate on the table. She seemed unfazed by this latest insult; in fact, she almost expected it. She reached for a piece of her confection and took a defeated bite. Then her face lit up, as if she were impressed by her own sweet self.

Later that evening, Adam and Steve decided they should sleep over at Adam's, thanks to the new tenant across the street from Steve's loft. Adam's Hell's Kitchen tenement was not nearly as fancy or luxurious as Steve's loft, but it did have one thing—curtains over Adam's one little window.

Adam lay on his bed, replaying the highlights of the disastrous evening in his mind. *Cornholers. Cocksuckers.* These words repeated in his mind like scratches on an old LP. Steve closed the curtains, just in case.

"Ugh. I'm never having sex again," Adam moaned.

Steve sat on the bed next to Adam and began to remove his cuff links.

"Oh, they'll be fine," Steve said. "They really liked you."

Adam leaned onto his elbow, facing his man. "As your dad was leaving, he told me I was going to hell."

"Well, he only tries to save the people he likes," Steve replied in all seriousness. He emptied his pockets onto the bedside table and began to go through his usual ritual of undressing. He had spent enough time at Adam's by this point to have developed a sense of entitlement toward the apartment. As he laid his keys and cell phone on the bedside table, he noticed for the first time that Adam's apartment contained no personal photographs of either himself or anyone else.

"Hey, how come I never hear about your parents?" Steve asked. "Are they in the witness protection program or something?"

Adam froze. He knew that this would come up eventually. He chose his words carefully while he looked at Steve. "Um, well," he said. "My parents are kind of weird."

"Weird like the kind of people who would raise a mime-fucker?" Steve asked with a teasing smile.

Adam laughed at Steve's joke; he knew Adam very well.

"No," Adam said. "They're kind of cursed. They're unlucky."

Steve had heard Adam talk often about luck since they met. He rolled his eyes. "Adam, there is no such thing as luck."

Adam gave Steve a wizened look. "Uh, yeah, there is actually. Listen, if you want to meet them, you can come with me to Hanukkah dinner next month—if you still like me."

Steve arched his eyebrows. "If I still *like* you?" he asked.

"Yeah, well, I'm just making an assumption there," Adam said, smiling.

Steve sat cross-legged on the bed, took Adam's hand in his, and gazed warmly into Adam's eyes. "I more than like you, Adam," he said.

Adam bit his lip. *Uh-oh—here it comes."*

"Adam, I—"

"I love you!" Adam blurted.

Steve put his head in his hands, then playfully punched Adam on the leg.

"You just had to say it first, didn't you?" Steve said in mock anger.

"I know. I'm sorry," Adam said. "It's easier for me to *say* it than *hear* it."

Steve knew how to proceed with this information. He laid on the most cornball romantic affectation in the world and slowly crawled on top of Adam, a syrup of mock sincerity dripping from his tongue. "I *loooove* you, Adam Bernstein! Oh, my God, I love, love, love *yooooooou!*"

Adam put his hands over his ears, and Steve tried to pull them off.

"I love you, I love you, I love you, I love you!" Steve moaned as Adam pretended to be in agony. But he wasn't.

He was in love, and so was Steve, and for two men to find love in New York City—well, that was just lovely. They held each other for a long time as the cells of their bodies settled into a harmonious rhythm. They wanted to remember this moment forever.

Chapter Eleven

The next day, Michael woke up to an empty apartment. This was getting old—this Adam thing. Why hadn't they broken up yet? For years Michael had known Steve as a career bachelor. This gay-love thing was ruining all their fun.

Michael stumbled to the kitchen; his pot hangover was particularly strong. He crept over to another pot—for coffee—then realized he didn't know how the machine worked. Steve had always made the coffee. Steve had always been there. But now that he was at Adam's all the time, Michael was having to learn how to be an adult—something that simply could not happen if Michael had any say in the matter. He stood and looked at the emptiness of the loft as if he were standing on a mountaintop, surveying the vastness of the world and feeling very small in comparison.

As the day went by, Michael went through his usual routine: He played video games, watched porn, ate Doritos, and passed gas. Somehow these things just weren't as fun without Steve around to ridicule him. Without Steve, Michael wasn't able to defend his behavior, so his behavior just seemed pathetic and stinky. As the sun set, he went to the kitchen counter and began rolling a joint with a piece of scrap paper. He had waited all day to call Steve, and he could wait no more.

He dialed Steve's cell phone, only to get a new outgoing voice message: "Hi, this is Steve. I am ridiculously in love and therefore extremely unreachable. But leave a message and I'll get back to you."

Michael thought about leaving a message, but what could he say? *I miss you? I'm lonely? I have no other friends?* None of these things seemed appropriate for a straight guy, so he hung up and went back to his joint rolling. As he finished, he took the scrap paper and dumped the leftover pot back into its small plastic cube when suddenly he saw something. The scrap paper was a flier for Rhonda's comedy act. It featured her holding a knife menacingly over her head. The caption KILLER COMEDY! ran beneath this menacing image. Michael looked at the address for Lou's Laf Attax" in Times Square. He got an idea. The Grinch got a terrible, awful, *wonderful* idea.

When Michael got to Lou's, the place was unusually packed. The unsavory-looking crowd seemed populated with men who were either homeless or made it a point to look dispossessed. Earlier that day, Lou had enlisted his alcoholic waitress, Miranda, to hand out fliers for the club. He put her in a suggestive outfit that revealed as much of her boobs as the public decency laws would allow. Naturally, she had attracted a certain kind of clientele that night—namely, gentlemen who might be more inclined to frequent a strip joint or a venue with live sex acts. Michael took a seat and ordered a drink from the barely conscious Miranda, who was three sheets— and a duvet—to the wind. All evening she had been stealing sips from drinks before she served them—an occupational hazard for her.

Lou took the stage in obscenely tight pants. His not-very-impressive package was blatantly visible through the white polyester, which acted as a kind of obscene shrink-wrap. Just moments before, he had been in his office, doing blow and masturbating to a Barbie Twins calendar—from 1998.

Lou stood before the crowd with a shit-eating grin on his face. Above his too-tight pants he wore the jacket of a track-suit, which was zipped way down to expose the ten strands of hair on his chest that fought for attention.

"All right," he began, "this next comic used to be really fat—which means that now her pussy is probably really tight since no one's ever been in there. She's the hottest female comic this side of, well, I can't think of any good-lookin' comics. But trust me, if you don't think she's funny—and she's not—just turn her around. I give you Rhonda Gernon and her amazing heart-shaped ass."

The shifty crowd drunkenly clapped as a furious Rhonda stormed the stage. Lou stepped off the stage and into the audience, where he leaned on a column with his arms folded across his chest. He was very pleased with himself.

Rhonda stood at the mike. *Should I? Yeah, why not?*

"Wow, what an introduction," she said. "You know Lou, I've always known you were crazy, but in those tight pants I can see you're nuts."

Lou's self-satisfied smile faded, and he tried not to draw attention to himself.

"And they're sad because there's no one up there. No pork, just beans. No sausage for your country breakfast. No condiments for your meat. No sauce. No relish. Lou's so small—ask me how small he is."

None of the men responded. They were confused by Rhonda's rant, which seemed less like comedy and more like castrating performance art. Michael, however, took the bait.

"How small is he?" he shouted.

"Thank you for asking," Rhonda cried. "Lou is so small, his last girlfriend was a pencil sharpener."

No one laughed except Michael. He laughed loudly and conspicuously as Miranda stumbled over with his drink. She sat it on his table, then drunkenly sat in his lap. Her eyes were crossed in an inebriated fashion. Usually, Michael would have leaped at the chance to seduce a big-boobed waitress, but he was too intrigued by Rhonda to reciprocate.

"Lou's so small," Rhonda continued, "he doesn't get crabs, he dates 'em!" Lou was fuming as the men in the audience turned to stare at him. The idea that this former fat girl could emasculate him—turn the tables on him—had never occurred to him in all the months he had sexually harassed her since her rapid weight loss. "If Lou were a drink, he'd be a 'no-piña' colada," Rhonda said, giggling to herself. She usually laughed at her own jokes out of nervousness, but tonight she was finally making jokes that were actually funny. Her anger had unleashed something that had lain dormant for years: her talent.

"Knock, knock!" she shouted at the mute audience.

Michael was fending off Miranda as she tried to drunkenly grab his crotch. "Who's there?" he shouted back to Rhonda.

Rhonda pantomimed looking for something with a magnifying glass. "Oh, I don't see anything. I guess it's Lou's penis."

Michael laughed uproariously, while the rest of the audience sat in a dazed stupor. Rhonda noticed the conspicuous laugher in the back of the room. "Well, at least there's one person in this audience secure enough with his masculinity to laugh at my jokes."

With that, all the men in the comedy club burst into forced nervous laughter. Rhonda put her hand over her eyes to see who had been laughing all along. To her surprise and horror, she saw that it was Michael, that awful little man from Steve's party. She also saw Miranda climbing on top of him and writhing around. Then she locked eyes with the one person who wasn't laughing—Lou. Lou was most certainly not amused.

An hour later, Michael stood by the exit, waiting for Rhonda to emerge after the show. Miranda was with him, still inebriated and still trying to paw him. At this point Michael had begun to regard her as a sort of annoying mosquito buzzing around him.

Rhonda emerged from backstage and approached Michael.

"Hey," she said. "Thanks for coming—and laughing."

"Oh, well, yeah, hey, wow—you know, you are really funny," Michael chuckled, remembering her act.

Rhonda seemed depressed. "Yeah, well, I just got fired," she said.

The drunken Miranda mustered up enough sobriety to formulate words.

"All Lou did was compliment you on your ass," she said. "Why'd you make fun of him?"

Rhonda looked at the drunken floozy in disbelief.

"Because in this 'heart-shaped ass' lies an asshole—which is, I guess, what I am."

Michael laughed at this image.

"That's gross," Miranda belched.

Rhonda had had enough and turned to leave. "Well, it's good to see you, Michael," she said. "Have fun with Gloria Steinem here."

As Rhonda walked away from the club, Michael ran after her. Rhonda threw up her skinny arm, attempting to hail a cab. But it was nearly eleven P.M., and the streets were bustling with tourists emptying out of the Times Square theaters.

"Hey, I wasn't with her. She just sat next to me," Michael cried over the hubbub.

"I'm not your mother," Rhonda croaked, scanning the dense traffic for a vacant cab.

"Oh, well, you kinda look like her," Michael said.

Rhonda couldn't believe how clueless this guy was. "Well, that's nice. Look, I'm late. There's a black hole I have to stare into, so if you don't mind…"

Michael decided to confess the real reason he had come

uptown that night. "I don't see Steve anymore since he hooked up with Adam. I think they're completely wrong for each other—don't you agree?"

This snapped Rhonda to attention. She had opinions about this subject. She lowered her arm and turned to look at Michael.

"Oh, come on, they're fags," she said. "You know how it is. Besides, I think it's good. Adam's luck has completely changed since they met and—ugh, why am I talking to you?" Rhonda looked back toward the oncoming traffic on Broadway. She considered just giving up and walking to the subway, but something was making her stay.

Michael stared at her. Something about Rhonda was remarkably attractive. She was actually quite beautiful but not in a way that Michael usually appreciated. She was classically beautiful as opposed to porn-beautiful.

"Hey, um, you wanna get a drink? It's so early," he said.

Rhonda scrunched her nose at him and shook her head. "I try not to drink," she said.

"Don't you get thirsty?" he asked.

"Booze—it's the carbs," Rhonda snapped. Michael recoiled like a scolded puppy.

"Oh, right, sorry," he said. Then he got an idea. "Are there carbohydrates in pot?"

It had been a long time since Rhonda had done drugs. She had tried coke with Adam in the '80s, and while it had been fun that first night, she had wanted to kill herself the next day. Her first coke hangover confirmed her suspicions that any drug that causes appetite suppression must be inherently evil. Marijuana, on the other hand, was a different story. She quite liked pot and had even used it to inspire her comedy writing when she was obese. Lately, though, times had been tough, and she couldn't afford luxury items like recreational drugs. Also, since Adam had gotten sober six months ago, Rhonda had pretty much followed suit. For better or worse, Rhonda was a world-class codependent.

But tonight Adam was with Steve—his new codependent. Now that he had a boyfriend, Adam didn't need Rhonda the way he used to. It did occur to her that Michael and she did have this in common; the only difference was that she thought it was a good thing. She thought Michael's pot was a good thing too, as she lifted the bong to her mouth in Steve's apartment. She sat at the foot of the gray sectional while Michael looked on from the couch. Uncomfortable with silence, he grabbed the remote and turned on the television where a soft-core porno was playing on one of the cable channels. Two party hat–titted pseudo-lesbians were bumping their fake breasts together in what appeared to be a commercial for a phone sex company.

"Wow, public access," Michael chuckled. "Can you believe they get away with that?"

Rhonda looked up at the screen, then looked back at Michael, whose belly was hanging out of his PICKLES DO IT WITH RELISH! T-shirt. She decided she was much too sober for this, so she turned back to the bong and took another long hit.

Michael, sensing her disapproval, jabbed at the remote, changing the channel. "Moon River" from *Breakfast at Tiffany's* began to play quietly on the TV.

"Hey, look—American Movie Classics. You like that, don't you?" he asked desperately.

Rhonda put the bong down and coughed. She was suitably stoned now. *Thank God.* "Isn't it funny how the only requirement for a movie to be a classic is that it be over forty years old?" she mused.

Michael smiled, "I never thought of that. Ha," he giggled. "You're funny. *Funny Lady.*"

Rhonda's stoned eyes lit up. She spun around to face him. "Oh, my God! I love that movie!"

"Hey, me too. Steve makes me watch it all the time—although I think *Funny Girl* is much more satisfying."

Rhonda turned and watched the movie, going back into her shell.

"Well, I think that's the common opinion," she said.

Michael and Rhonda watched the old movie for a very long time. Not being adept at the small talk necessary for seduction, they just stared at the TV screen. Rhonda started thinking about the first time she saw *Breakfast at Tiffany's*. Most girls watched that classic film and drooled over the diamonds Audrey Hepburn admired in the window of the famed jewelry shop at dawn. When Rhonda had watched that scene, she had drooled over the Danish Miss Hepburn held. The scene was just another example of how images of food were misrepresented to the American public, Rhonda concluded. Audrey Hepburn never ate Danish pastry. She was too skinny to eat Danish. Then Rhonda thought, *Wait a minute. Is Audrey Hepburn Danish? She has that strange unidentifiable accent.* Rhonda remembered reading something about how Audrey Hepburn had been in a concentration camp. Or had she just been living in Europe during World War II? Rhonda couldn't remember exactly, but suddenly she realized she was stoned, and her train of thought was becoming that of a stoned person on marijuana.

Her spell was broken when Michael stood. "Wow, I've got the munchies," he declared.

Rhonda barely registered this as Michael went to the kitchen. He opened the refrigerator and removed a large chocolate-cream pie, then pulled two enormous spoons from a drawer. When he returned from the kitchen and Rhonda spied him, her red-rimmed eyes bulged.

"What're you doing? I can't eat that," she yelped, her hands covering her mouth.

"What? You can't even have one piece of pie?" Michael asked coyly.

"No, I can't have one pie. One piece of pie is like an appetizer to me. I eat that, I unleash the beast."

This turned Michael on. "Well, then come on, Rhonda," he said huskily. "Unleash the beast."

Michael walked over to Rhonda and sat near her on the couch. He put the pie in his crotch and spread his legs. Rhonda bit her lip.

"I know you want it," he cooed. The struggle in Rhonda was immense. She chewed on her hand to try to satisfy her burning hunger. She hadn't had pie in so long. She hadn't had penis in much longer. Not knowing what to do, Rhonda decided she wanted to have her pie and eat penis too. She pushed the pie into Michael's stunned face, then knocked him back on the couch, devouring him and the pie. Both of them began to lick the sweet filling off each other's faces, necks, and crotches. When they were done, Rhonda ran to the fridge for more—because one pie was too many and a thousand never enough.

The next day, Adam and Steve visited Chinatown and picked up the custom-made blinds for Steve's loft. They knew there was nothing they could do legally to silence the guy across the street. Over the last week they had both come up with horrible fantasies about how they could kill him or humiliate him. Adam joked that perhaps they could kidnap him, dress him in a tutu, and hire a big steroidal muscleman to come over and pound his butt. Steve thought of videotaping the scene and selling copies at the local deli for all the neighbors to see. But once they had exhausted all of their highly creative revenge fantasies, they decided not to pursue any of them. They simply got the blinds and walked to Steve's apartment to install them.

As they entered the loft, they were being very lovey-dovey, kissing and canoodling. Then, as they entered the main living area, Adam noticed Steve's face drop. He looked down and saw a huge mess on the floor. Potato chips, cookies, and empty cake-frosting containers littered a path that ran from the kitchen to the bedroom.

Adam and Steve followed the trail of food and found Rhonda and Michael in Steve's bed. They were both covered with the sticky remnants of food and sex. Michael's face had been licked clean. His hair had been slurped into a perfect point atop his forehead—not a cowlick—a Rhonda-lick.

Rhonda stirred, sensing eyes on her. She pried her eyes open; she had a deep hangover from the pot and insulin rush the night before. She saw Adam and knew she was busted, but she didn't care.

"I had a slip," she said sheepishly. Then she laid her head back down and went to sleep again, her hunger deeply satisfied, and her belly full of Michael.

Chapter Twelve

As Adam and Steve got off the train in Montauk, Long Island, Adam was shivering not only because of the deplorable, cold December air but also the case of nerves induced by the looming introduction of Steve to his parents.

While Steve hailed the cab that would take them the twenty or so miles to the Bernsteins' house, Adam stood shivering both inside and out. He'd never introduced his parents to any boyfriend. In truth, Adam had never had a boyfriend, although he had come out to his parents years ago in junior high school. It was 1979, and the local PBS station had decided to air the bodybuilding documentary *Pumping Iron* one dark and rainy night. Adam had seen the advertisements and had secretly planned on watching what to him seemed like soft-core pornography—piped right into his bedroom and onto his tiny black and white TV. At two A.M. he quietly moved to the set and turned it on. Arnold Schwarzenegger's muscles filled the screen as Adam's penis filled the crotch of his polyester pajamas. Just as he began to masturbate, his father and mother threw open the door, catching him red-handed—literally.

Instead of admonishments, Adam's parents flung their arms around their boy and promised to love him no matter what. His parents had always been so unconditionally accepting and loving that sometimes he almost wished they were like normal parents who would shame him for who he was. Instead, he had to deal with his folks trying to set him up on dates with other gays they knew. His mother's hairdresser was one potential suitor, as was the son of his father's proctologist. Perhaps it was out of guilt that his parents were so accepting. They knew they had given their son some distinct disadvantages in this life—the Bernstein curse being one of them.

Moments after they stepped out of the cab, Adam stormed up the pathway to his family's ranch-style suburban home, complete with an American flag guarding the front porch. The front yard was barren and neglected; just a few shrubs were left to their own devices on the lawn. This was definitely the home of people who didn't care for yard work.

Steve followed Adam, who stopped him at the front door.

"I don't think this is a good idea," Adam groaned nervously.

"Oh, come on. You met my parents. I want to meet yours." Steve had gotten used to neurotic outbursts such as this from his boyfriend. By now he took them in stride.

"All I'm saying is—" Adam continued.

"I know, I know: They're not lucky," Steve said wearily.

"They're kind of cursed," Adam said, punctuating this sentence with a furrowed brow.

"Adam, stop it. Now focus. Relax, you always exaggerate everything." Steve took Adam by the shoulders and nudged him. "Now go. Go in."

Adam knew it was no use. These were his parents, like it or not, and Steve would meet them and either break up with Adam on the spot or break up with him later after they left.

Adam and Steve entered the modest home. Immediately, Steve noticed that the foyer was decked with festive Hanukkah decorations. Hanukkah ornaments and Stars of David covered every available surface. Steve, who was completely unaccustomed to this Jewish holiday, took it all in.

"Hello? We're here," Adam shouted.

Just then Steve noticed a woman standing in the middle of a neat and cozy country-themed living room. She spun around to face them, and Steve saw that the woman was wearing what appeared to be a contraption used to treat people with broken necks. A halo, Steve remembered it was called. The woman was dressed in a simple blue skirt and long-sleeve dress shirt that he could tell she thought of as fancy. She seemed elated to see them.

"Oh! Welcome home!" she cried jubilantly.

Just then, a glass light fixture on the ceiling wobbled and came off its screws, crashing onto the woman's head and shattering into a million pieces. Steve was taken completely aback by this horrible accident. Suddenly. he realized that the woman was indeed Adam's mother.

"Darn it. We just had that replaced last week," she chuckled, barely fazed by this incident. Adam also acted as if nothing had happened, and he strolled over to hug his mom.

"Happy Hanukkah," he said as he hugged her. Small pieces of glass flecked in her hair.

Steve stepped farther into the room but stopped when he heard the sound of a motor whirring somewhere. Everyone turned to see a middle-aged man come flying around the corner in a motorized wheelchair. He pulled up alongside Steve and stuck out his hand.

"Welcome, welcome. You must be Steve. I'm Norm, Adam's father. And this is Sherry, my wife, and here's our beautiful daughter, Ruth."

A young woman rose from the plastic-covered couch and approached Adam and Steve. She was about thirty, and her right arm was in a large cast that was supported by a metal rod attached to a belt around her hip.

"Hi. Very nice to meet—ah!" Ruth's face scrunched up into a portrait of pain and embarrassment. Blood filled her mouth.

"Uh-oh. Bite your tongue again, sweetie?" Norm asked.

Ruth nodded as her mother instinctively handed her a Kleenex to wipe her bleeding mouth.

Steve stood and looked at the members of Adam's family of origin. They were all grinning from ear to ear. He guessed they rarely, if ever, had visitors of any kind. They were so happy and cheerful. Then Steve noticed that the living room seemed to have been childproofed. Every sharp corner or jagged edge of furniture had been covered in plastic bubble wrap. The corners of the fireplace mantle were covered in pink foam insulation, and the furniture and floor were covered in shiny plastic. They were the family in the plastic bubble. Nevertheless, they couldn't have been warmer to Steve.

"Hello, Ruth, Mr. and Mrs. Bernstein. Thanks so much for having me," Steve said.

Sherry chimed in. "Oh, please, call me Sherry," she said. Any boyfriend of Adam's is a boyfriend of mine."

"That's right," Norm laughed. "It's been kinda hard getting this one to come and visit once in a while. I think he's just a little embarrassed by the Bernstein curse."

Adam remembered that Steve had said there was no such thing as luck. Maybe he was right. Maybe this was one big self-fulfilling prophecy. Adam looked at his father.

"Dad, there is no such thing," he said.

Adam looked at Steve triumphantly, then walked over to a chair, sat down, and went flying backward. Everyone looked at him knowingly.

The Bernsteins couldn't stop staring at Steve as they ate their holiday meal. Steve was so dashing, so handsome—such a shiksa god. Adam had done so well. Norm sat at the head of the dining room table across from his wife, and Ruth faced Adam and Steve.

"Steve, would you like some matzos?" Norm asked.

"Yes, thank you very much."

With that, Norm lifted a "grabber" arm complete with claw and handle from beside his chair. He grabbed some flat bread and very clumsily passed it to Steve. Everyone acted as if this was perfectly normal. Steve chuckled, realizing where Adam got his clumsy charm.

They continued to eat. Suddenly, a large mirror behind Norm lost its grip on the wall and crashed to the floor, where it loudly shattered into a million splinters.

Norm barely looked up from his soup. "Woops. Seven more," he said.

Sherry took in the mess. "Huh. They told me that was shatterproof."

At this point Steve had to say something. How could he not? This was beyond anything he had ever witnessed. It was as if he had entered the Bermuda Triangle—the Bernstein Triangle. "I'm sorry, but I just have to ask—are all of you okay with this?"

Everyone smiled. Adam froze, nervous that Steve would judge him and his family. Norm put down his fork and started to hold court.

"You know, Steve, I used to charge folks a quarter every time they asked us that, but no one could afford it. Lowered it to a nickel, and it still practically broke everyone's bank. Happiness is accepting life on life's terms, no matter what they happen to be. You just do your best with what you've been given."

Adam looked at Steve nervously. Steve smiled.

Sherry leaned toward Steve to elaborate. "Till we found out we were luck-challenged, we thought there was a poltergeist in the house."

"We were on *In Search Of* in the '70s—you know, with Spock?" Ruth said, smiling.

Sherry lit up at this comment. "Oooh! We've still got the tape," she said. "We can watch it right after we light the menorah."

Adam put his hands on his face. "Mom, can we please get through Hanukkah without watching that damn tape," he said.

"Adam doesn't like that tape," Norm cracked. "He was a real pizza face back then."

"Too busy with all that white face paint to let it clear," Sherry teased. "Would anyone like some coffee?"

With that Sherry bounded up from the table to go to the kitchen. Steve looked at Adam confusedly. "White face paint?" he asked.

"I was a goth in high school," Adam explained.

Several days later, Steve was still thinking about the Bernsteins. Lying next to his boyfriend, Steve watched Adam sleep. He studied his face, quietly watching Adam dream, wondering about all the things Adam had seen in his life and wishing he had been there for more of it. Adam's family was so accepting—so utterly unlucky yet so completely wonderful and loving in a way that his own parents had never been. Steve had spent many years counseling damaged people. He had begun to wonder if hardship really did build character, as some believe. Usually, it seemed to him that damaged people were not better off because of their damage, but in Adam's case the opposite seemed true. Adam's family had endured hardships most people would have been unable to bear. Steve gazed at his boyfriend and felt overwhelming love for him. As eccentric as Adam was, Steve had finally discovered what it was about Adam that made him so lovable. Adam was brave. He had saved himself from a lot in life—something that only a good shrink might have noticed. Steve gently brushed the hair off Adam's face, kissing his forehead and the dreams that lay inside his complicated noggin.

The next day Steve stopped by Marie's Crisis downstairs. He found Rhonda busy prepping the bar while Michael sat on a stool and watched her work. Steve still wasn't quite sure what he thought of this odd couple's burgeoning romance. The fact that Michael was having a romance with someone besides a toothless street prostitute both shocked and relieved him. Perhaps Rhonda's presence in Michael's life would cushion the blow that Steve was about to deliver.

"Why can't a lesbian diet and put on makeup at the same time?" Rhonda asked in her best comedy stage persona.

Michael gleefully played along. "I don't know. Why?" he asked.

" 'Cause you can't eat Jenny Craig with Mary Kay on your face."

Rhonda cracked up. She was used to laughing at her own jokes when no one else would. But someone else was laughing now. Michael howled with delight while Steve put his hands in his face, embarrassed.

"Does anyone know what 'moth balls' smell like?" Rhonda asked, her comedy face twisted in a smirk.

"Yes," Michael blurted.

"Oh, really? How'd you get them to spread their little legs?" Rhonda asked.

Rhonda and Michael roared. Rhonda turned to a stone-faced Steve.

"I have an audition for a lesbian cruise ship next week," Rhonda reported. "Very excited about it. I like lesbians; lesbians like me. I'm trying to cut down on the fat jokes, though."

Steve looked at Rhonda appraisingly. "I still can't imagine you fat," he said.

Michael perked up. "Oh, I can," he said. "Hey, honey, show Steve that photo of yourself."

Michael reached for Rhonda's purse and searched for an old photo of Rhonda. The photo was of Rhonda and Adam as their '80s goth personae. She always carried it with her as a reminder of who she had been in her former life. Anytime she felt like eating fast food, she pulled out the picture— a ritual that often caused her to dissolve into tears and run to an Overeaters Anonymous meeting. Michael found the photo and was about to hand it to Steve when Rhonda intervened, taking it away from Michael.

"No. I look like a Long Island blimp with a bad Chinese-lady perm. No!" She snatched the picture away and returned it to her wallet. Steve took a sip of the beer he had ordered.

"Speaking of Long Island," he said, "Adam and I went there recently—to his parents' house."

Rhonda stopped and turned to Steve dramatically. "Oh, my God," she said. "I was there once, and a piece of Sky Lab splashed down into their pool."

Steve couldn't help but laugh. *Of course it did,* he thought. He settled onto his barstool, then looked at Michael and Adam's best friend. He took a breath. This was a big moment.

"I'm going to ask Adam to marry me," he said.

"Oh, my God!" Rhonda exclaimed joyously.

"Oh, my God!" Michael exclaimed miserably. "Marry him? But you guys have only been going out for a couple of months."

"Actually, it's been almost a year, Michael," Steve said testily. "And besides, my parents got married on their third date, and they're still together."

"Well, people are only as monogamous as their options," Michael observed. "Your parents live in a trailer park in a field."

Rhonda took this and ran. Her jaw dropped. "Excuse me?" she said. "Only as monogamous as their options?"

Steve forged ahead. He knew this would be hard for Michael since they had been in a sort of "dry marriage" to each other. They had all the codependency and enmeshment of a typical husband and wife, only without the good stuff—like sex.

"It gets worse, Michael," Steve said. "I'm going to ask Adam to move in."

"Oh, my God—oh! I *knew* this day would come." Michael cried in dismay.

Rhonda and Steve looked at this little man with the beer belly in mild astonishment.

"Michael, you said you needed a place to crash, and you've been living on my couch for five years," Steve said.

Michael grunted and muttered under his breath like an old man.

"Jesus, Michael, be happy for them," Rhonda admonished. She turned warmly to Steve. "I, for one, think it's great. He's going to flip out. He *really* loves you."

Steve smiled. "I love him too," he said. "I do. It's funny—when I was a kid, I thought I'd grow up and have a big wedding. It turned out I was gay, and I just figured it wasn't in the cards. I don't know. I'm not sure how I even feel about marriage. Sometimes it seems like a dying institution."

"Well, it is," Rhonda cracked, "but then you fall in love."

Touched by this moment, Michael placed his hand lovingly on Rhonda's arm. She slapped it, and he recoiled in pain.

Then Steve continued, lost deep in thought. "Sometimes I look at him and think, *Wow, this is not the person I was supposed to wind up with.* But somehow it's okay. It's more than okay."

Rhonda smiled and shared a moment with Steve. She touched his arm supportively, and her eyes welled up. After all these years of watching her friend struggle just to keep his head above the waters of self-inflicted drama, now she was going to give him away as his maid of honor.

Michael broke the spell with a loud beer-induced belch.

"So who gets to wear the dress?" he asked.

"You do," Rhonda snapped.

The next day, Steve went in search of a ring. He wasn't sure where a man might go to purchase such a thing for another man, so he did what many gay men in New York do when faced with such a quandary—he went to the ghetto, Chelsea. He knew of a gay-owned shop there that sold wedding bands. Michael, feeling suitably ashamed of his recent disapproval of the proposed wedding, tagged along to help.

As they walked into a store called Jack's Off Sixth, Michael noticed the wide array of items for purchase. Featuring everything from barrels of Elbow Grease to scented candles and potpourri, Jack's Off was potpourri itself of gay-themed consumables. Here you could purchase a wedding band for your male lover and also a penis-enlarging pump for your wedding night. The millions of confusing items overwhelmed Michael. Steve, however, was used to these conflicting images of gayness. Somewhere in him was a cokehead penis pumper. But these days he was playing the part of another kind of gay men—the kind that gets married.

Steve approached the sales counter, where a very militant-looking gay employee stood at attention. In his mid thirties with a "faux-hawk" and various tattoos and piercings, the store clerk had obviously put great effort into turning his body into a walking advertisement of studied queerness. He wore a T-shirt stating I CAN'T EVEN THINK STRAIGHT!

"Hi, I was wondering if you could help us?" Steve asked.

The salesclerk affected a New York gay-fashionista smile of superiority.

"That's why I'm here," he said smugly.

"Well, I want to buy a ring."

The salesclerk didn't miss a beat. "Cock, pride, nipple, or finger?" he asked.

Steve blinked his eyes. "Finger? A wedding band," he said.

The salesclerk's entire demeanor changed suddenly. Perky turned into prickly pretty quickly. "Oh, I see," he said coolly.

With that, he reached under the counter, removed a tray of wedding bands, and slammed them down loudly in front of a stunned Steve and Michael. "And which one of you is the lucky woman?"

Steve barely knew how to respond. "Excuse me?" he said.

"Well, I was just wondering. I mean, you're copying straight culture and all, buying into the institution of enslavement of another person, turning back all that hard-won sexual liberation we've earned over the years. I was just wondering which of you is the woman."

Steve's blood boiled. This guy didn't even know Adam or him. To be reduced to some kind of abstraction infuriated him. He was about to respond when Michael suddenly spoke up. "I'm the woman," he said.

Both Steve and the salesclerk arched their eyebrows and looked at the sheepish straight guy with a beer belly and five o'clock shadow.

"Yeah, 'cause when you're a gay, one's always the man and one's always the woman, right? I can't help it. One look at this one, and my legs go skyward—total helium heels."

About an hour later, Steve and Michael stood outside the famous Tiffany's off Fifth, admiring the jewels in the window.

"What're you gonna tell them?" Michael asked.

Steve rolled his eyes, then looked inside at the elderly men working behind the counter.

"Oh, please. This place is just as gay as that store in Chelsea. But older queens tend to be a little more romantic."

Steve went inside, and Michael stood watching. He saw Steve approach a well-dressed older gentleman who stood behind the ring counter. Steve seemed to be explaining what he needed. Suddenly, the older gentleman burst into gleeful tears, reached over, and hugged Steve excitedly.

Later, Steve sat in his loft holding the wedding band, lost in thought. All his life he had wanted to get married, and now he had found the person he wanted to share the rest of his life with. In his mind he rehearsed what he would say when Adam came home. He had thought about getting down on one knee to propose in one of their favorite restaurants. He had thought about hiding the ring in a dessert but knew that Adam would be likely to swallow it, given his luck-challenged condition. Then he got an even more majestic idea. He would take Adam someplace very grand. He wanted the proposal to be sweeping and epic and memorable and so New York.

Just then the door opened and Adam came in, keys jangling. Steve quickly snapped the ring case shut and hid it away in his coat pocket.

Adam approached, happy to see his boyfriend.

"Hey, good-lookin'," Adam said, walking up to Steve and kissing him hello. He was about to walk away, but Steve held his arm and pulled him back, embracing him and looking intensely into his eyes. Adam smiled, surprised at this gesture. Steve kissed Adam romantically for a long time.

"Listen, I want to take you someplace," Steve whispered.

Adam's heart sank. "Oh, no. Please don't tell me there's something called three-stepping."

Steve chuckled. "No, just my favorite place in the city. You game?"

Adam was confused. Steve was acting really weird. Steve never acted weird; that was Adam's job. Nevertheless, Adam nodded and off they went.

In the cab Steve couldn't stop smiling. Adam was completely confused and wondered what this trip could possibly mean. It was in Adam's nature always to suspect the worst was just about to happen. He wondered if Steve was taking him somewhere to tell him that he had cancer or AIDS or maybe that he had murdered someone. But then he saw that goofy grin on Steve's face.

When they got out of the cab, Adam and Steve took in the East River and the mammoth structure above it.

"The Brooklyn Bridge?" Adam said. "That's your favorite place?"

"Yeah. Come on." Steve grabbed Adam and excitedly tickled him. Then he took Adam's hand and led him toward the walkway.

It was a cold winter day as they walked onto the historic landmark, completely unaware of the bit of their own history they were repeating. Bicyclists and joggers greeted and passed them. The bridge was bustling with activity in spite of the weather, with plucky New Yorkers drinking in the crisp winter sunshine. Steve put his arm around Adam and led him to the uppermost peak of the bridge. They stopped and gazed down on lower Manhattan. It was a beautiful clear view.

"Wow. I haven't been here in years. It's so weird to see downtown without the towers," Adam said.

Steve turned to Adam. He was suddenly serious.

"You were here on that day. What was it like?"

"I don't know," Adam said. "It was just so…sad."

Steve saw an opening. He was so nervous and wanted to say just the right thing.

"These are scary times, Adam. It makes things like security and commitment more important."

Adam was touched. He kissed Steve and held him as they gazed out at the skyscrapers wedged between centuries-old buildings. Adam felt like talking. So he did.

"I can't believe you brought me here," he said. "My drug problem began on this very spot. Well, actually it began at Danceteria, this nightclub in the '80s."

Steve pretended to laugh and nodded, as if he knew of this place from a long time ago. Adam continued: "This go-go boy cokehead with big ol' Dee Snider hair fed me my first hit of blow. He was in some dance troupe—what were they called? Oh, the Dazzle Dancers! That's right. Well, we walked across the Brooklyn Bridge back to my place where he fed me more blow. Then he took a *shit* right in front of me—all over my carpet. Oh, my God! He was so disgusting. My place looked like something out of *Willy Wonka* after he left. Oh! And he was singing some song from some musical. What was it? *The Sound of Music,* that's it. God, how could I have forgotten that?"

As Steve listened, he felt his insides liquefy. He became a hollow shell of a human. All the love he felt for Adam evaporated in a matter of moments as he realized that Adam was that goth kid he had pooped on in 1987. Suddenly, the events of that night crystallized into total recall. He remembered that night more clearly than the last year with Adam. That night in the '80s suddenly seemed much more "real" than his current relationship with Adam. Steve broke out into a sweat. He was not that person anymore. When he turned to look at his boyfriend, though, Steve was not only that coked-out Dazzle Dancer, but Adam was also that highly unattractive goth freak. Steve's memory of that night had turned his stomach for a long time afterward. Eventually, he had blocked out any conscious recall of what had happened. And because he had blocked it out, he hadn't ever noticed that Adam was who he was.

"Oh, my God. Oh, my Jesus, my God!" Steve exclaimed.

He began to slowly back away from Adam, as if he were radioactive.

"Honey? Is something wrong?" Adam took a step toward the rapidly retreating shrink whom he loved.

"Adam, I have to get out of here," Steve cried. "All I can see is disaster—disaster!" Steve continued in retreat. Adam was completely confused and extremely concerned about Steve's emotional outburst and seeming nervous breakdown. "I need time to think, Adam—time to think."

With that Steve ran away, pulling a ten-year-old boy off his bicycle and riding away in a panic.

"Where are you going?" Adam called out, but it was too late. Steve was gone, speeding back to Manhattan and disappearing into eight million people.

Chapter Thirteen

The next day, after numerous unreturned phone calls to Steve, Adam met Rhonda for a yoga class at the Crunch gym in Hell's Kitchen. Adam was confused and upset, but because he was in recovery he was used to knowing people who flipped out from time to time, only to return when they were ready. While Steve's behavior had been rude, Adam was a pretty forgiving guy. He figured everyone was entitled to the occasional breakdown. He knew himself that eventually he would panic over something, and he would want Steve to be compassionate when that day arrived.

Showing up late, he joined the yoga class that was already in progress, dragging a mat next to Rhonda and jumping right into downward dog position. Rhonda turned her head to Adam.

"So he just ran away yelling 'disaster'?" she whispered.

"Yeah, we were on the Brooklyn Bridge talking about the World Trade Center and what had happened, and he just flipped out."

"Well, he'll come around. Everyone gets jitters right before—"

Rhonda realized she had said too much. She stomped

forward into plank pose to change the subject, out of step with the rest of the class. Adam followed her lead.

"Before what?" he asked.

Rhonda tried her best to cover up. "The next big terrorist attack," she said.

Adam thought this a strange change of subject. For the first time he wondered if Rhonda knew something he didn't about Steve. He began to wonder if Steve was seeing someone else and had taken Adam to the Brooklyn Bridge to tell him he was leaving, only to become overwhelmed and run away in fear. Adam thought about what Michael had told him about Steve being a slut. For the first time he began to wonder if he was deluding himself about Steve's love for him.

After Steve left the bridge, he entered a kind of time-warp trance that took him back to the days before he met Adam again. The doors slammed shut in his heart, and although he had heard Adam's messages, he took comfort in the daily rituals of his life, including his daily workout.

Sitting on the stationary bicycle, Steve spun his legs and held a personal motorized fan to keep his handsome face cool and dry. As he watched the television monitors, he did something he had become very good at—zoning out. His attention shifted, however, when a good-looking young man similar to Adam in coloring and build walked by and blatantly cruised him. Steve watched the young man coyly slip into the locker-room entrance, a signal he knew very well. He had ignored these signals during the last year while he was dating Adam. But today he needed to reassure himself that he was autonomous. And while he wasn't emotionally able to lay claim to his distant past, he needed to reclaim his not-so-distant behavior. He got up and entered the locker room in hot pursuit.

Moments later Steve had undressed and wandered to the shower area. He noticed the back and bare butt of the young man as he slipped into a shower stall. Steve licked his chops and slinked over to the hot guy who would afford him a much-needed fix. He slipped into the shower.

Inside, the young man shampooed his hair, his nicely muscled back to Steve. Steve moved stealthily toward the object of his erection and touched his shoulder. The young man gasped, shocked, then spun around. The young man was not a stranger but indeed Steve's boyfriend, Adam, who was showering after his yoga class with Rhonda.

When Adam and Steve saw each other, they shrieked like two B-movie actresses in a horror movie. Then they both instinctively covered their penises.

"It's you!" Steve blurted.

"It's me?" Adam replied. Soap was running into his eyes, and he squinted through the pain.

Steve was stumped: *How to proceed?* He was completely and utterly busted, and no attempt at covering this up would help.

"So, how have you been?" Steve asked, as if at a high school reunion.

"I've been—naked!" Adam squealed. They both felt completely exposed. Suddenly, Adam remembered what Michael told him about Steve's sordid past. "Oh, my God—you thought I was someone else," he said.

"No! No, Adam, of course not," Steve said.

"Where have you been? I've been calling. Did I do something wrong?"

Steve closed his eyes. Being a shrink, he knew that by rejecting Adam he was really rejecting parts of himself. But reject himself he did.

Rhonda sat in the lobby of Crunch reading her *New Yorker,* post–yoga workout, waiting for Adam. She didn't much like this gym. The music made her think of a rave party for people with jobs. She always carried her *New Yorker* as a sort of intelligent superhero weapon. When faced with an undesirable person, situation, or setting, she could bury her nose in its pages and zap people out of existence. She was reading a particularly infuriating essay on George W. Bush's recent blunders when suddenly Adam came running up. He was dressed, but his hair was wet and he seemed hysterical.

"He just dumped me," Adam cried.

Rhonda stood up like a codependent marine. "Oh, my God!" she exclaimed as she put her hand over her mouth.

"There ain't no God," Adam declared.

"Did he say why?" she asked.

Adam was in an adrenaline-fueled fight-or-flight mode. He struggled to remember the details of his breakup. It was as if Adam had just become a camera that had recorded the soul-damaging experience for posterity.

"Uh, he said he wasn't ready and I didn't really know who he was," Adam said.

Like any good friend, Rhonda acted as if this misfortune had happened to her personally. Her face became a portrait of soap-opera angst as her knees grew weak and she sat back down on her chair.

"Oh, my God! Why is this happening?" she shrieked at top volume. A gym is not a place one usually witnesses great human or personal drama. But not today. The lobby was filling with gym patrons running to see what the commotion was about.

Adam answered Rhonda's question with certain authority.

"It's the Bernstein curse," he cried. The he sat next to his best friend, only to have the chair collapse beneath him, sending him tumbling backward, legs going skyward. He lay on the floor blubbering as Rhonda went to help him up.

"Let's just get out of here," Rhonda said. Off they went onto Eighth Avenue, holding each other and weeping.

Adam's breakup had indeed ended his reprieve from the Bernstein curse. Over the course of the next week, everything happened to Adam—bad luck became a way of life again.

Chairs continued to break, soda cans exploded in his face, passing trucks splashed muddy water into his face, waitresses dropped entire trays of food on him. He accepted that this was his lot in life again, just as his parents had taught him. He continued to go to his Alcoholics Anonymous meetings—they were his only respite from the accidents and mishaps.

Rhonda watched all of this unfolding and felt powerless to do anything to stop the barrage. She met Adam at Amy's Bread in Hell's Kitchen for coffee and a "kitchen sink" cookie. While Adam stood outside, he remembered the time Steve and he had come to this bakery. It was one of the places that was most meaningful in his romance, and returning was a painful experience. When you fall in love in New York City every familiar street corner possesses the power to destroy you emotionally if your romance ends abruptly. Each subway entrance retains a memory of a shared glance, each storefront a stolen kiss—the city becomes a sort of three-dimensional scrapbook of lost love. As Adam stood outside Amy's, he began to cry. Rhonda joined him and went to hand him a cookie when suddenly his face contorted into a pinched grimace. Blood began to trickle out of his mouth. Like his sister, Ruth, Adam had bit his tongue. A horrified Rhonda handed her friend a napkin to tend to his injury, then held him for a long time. This was it. She'd had enough. Adam could bite his tongue, but she could bite hers no more.

Steve had shown up for work at St. Luke's worn-out and frustrated. He had been up all night with insomnia, wrestling with his decision to leave Adam, a decision that he ultimately decided was the right one to make. Michael had noticed something weird about Steve's behavior, especially when Steve ceremoniously opened the much-ballyhooed window blinds that blocked out the homophobe across the street.

Steve's first task of the day was counseling an attractive blond woman named Harriet. Still dressed in work clothes and sporting tennis shoes for the subway ride home, Harriet had shown up in the emergency room with her barking husband in tow. It seemed that she had come home from her Wall Street office to find her husband eating out of a bowl on the floor and scratching imaginary fleas with his hind legs. Not knowing what to do, she simply brought him to the ER. Steve counseled Harriet while her husband growled and barked in the next room.

"You know, you date," Harriet explained, her eyes brimming with tears. "You look for the person who you think has the least amount of flaws and is about as close to perfect as you can get—"

"Yes, but of course there's no such thing as perfection," Steve replied, in his best doctor mode. He held a clipboard with Harriet's husband's chart on it. He seemed interested, but his mind was really elsewhere.

"Why do people project this image of themselves that's like the opposite of who they really are?" she asked.

Steve looked at her with affected sympathy. "Perhaps they're worried that they won't be loved for who they really are," he said. As usual, Steve didn't see the irony in his comment. When he was working, he never saw himself or his own problems reflected in his patients, a precaution he had learned well in medical school.

"But that's crazy," Harriet replied. "I mean, you think you know this person, then you come home and realize you do not know this person from Adam."

This comment punctured Steve's professional veneer. He looked up at this woman and suddenly became transparent. His face grew slack.

There was a commotion in the adjoining waiting area, then Rhonda came flying through the doors Adam had burst through with Burt nearly a year ago. She approached the triage nurse.

"I need to speak to Steven Hicks," she demanded.

"Are you one of his patients?" the rather large African-American woman behind the desk asked.

"Don't make me go Shirley MacLaine on you, bitch!" Rhonda exclaimed.

Rhonda stormed into Steve's office. Steve leaped up to intercept her. Harriet turned and watched.

"You better give that guy some closure, or he's gonna wind up in here in a body cast," Rhonda declared.

Steve tried to quiet Rhonda's histrionics by whispering. "Rhonda," he hissed, "I appreciate you standing up for your friend, but I did give Adam closure."

"In a shower stall!" Rhonda cried. Steve desperately tried to quiet the very unsubtle stand-up comedienne. He gently put his hand over his own mouth as if to say *shh,* but Rhonda raged on. "One minute you're telling me you want to marry him—all this bullshit about commitment—and you're a total slut."

"Rhonda, listen, you don't know the whole story. There are things about me that you just don't know," Steve murmured.

"Like what?" Rhonda cried, exasperated.

Steve thought about just telling Rhonda who he was, but that would mean he also would have to admit he was once a messy cokehead, and he simply couldn't do that—especially at work, where he was supposed to be the healthy one.

"He didn't really love me," Steve said. "We were codependent and—"

Jumping on Steve's words, Rhonda's raised her voice to a shout.

"Well, there are good things about being cody," she said. "It's called depending on another person. You act like you're so grown-up, like you're so above it, but you're an asshole—and a baby. You're an asshole who's also a baby."

With that, Rhonda burst into tears and fled through the waiting room full of nutcases. Rhonda didn't mind being a nutcase—it afforded her all the freedoms that Steve wouldn't

143

allow himself. Harriet, who had been watching this unfolding drama, looked at Steve and rolled her eyes.

"I'm getting marriage advice from some gay whore—great," she said.

After this very public confrontation, Steve went home and went right to bed. Michael noticed something was up. Holding a bag of Chili Cheese Fritos, he walked into Steve's bedroom and stood staring at him. Steve's behavior made Michael feel insecure—the way a child might feel when his mommy is sick or going through something grown-up. Michael's crunching woke Steve from his fitful sleep.

Steve had thought about opening up to his one and only real friend. They didn't have the kind of relationship that supported hand-holding. But after Rhonda had confronted Steve, his ensuing confusion made him realize that perhaps this was the time to talk about what had happened. He sat up in bed and looked at his slobby roommate with expectation and resolve. Michael knew all the players in the drama. It was Michael or no one else.

Fifteen minutes later, Michael was lying next to Steve on the bed. They were both perfectly still.

"Okay, let me get this straight," Michael said. "You meet Adam in 1987. You turn him into a cokehead and then you poop on him—all in the same night?" Steve grimaced. Even discussing the situation was difficult. Then he remembered this was Michael—someone who slept with homeless women—and he felt better.

"It wasn't my fault," Steve said. "It was cut with baby laxative."

Michael took this in, trying to imagine the horror of that night. "Wow. I've had some bad dates but nothing like a biohazard."

Steve lay on the bed, staring up at the ceiling of his expensive loft. He thought about how he had reinvented himself after that night; how he would never have become a doctor, never have come to own his own place, if he hadn't fallen so low.

"How could we have dated for so long and never recognized each other?" Steve asked. This was the million-dollar question.

"Oh, it was the '80s. It was a long time ago," Michael said. His tone was almost comforting, a quality neither Steve nor he ever thought he possessed. But it didn't last. Michael's earnestness quickly dissolved into stupid straight-guy talk. "You were like Simon Le Bon in a boat, running through the jungle looking for that cat lady. And he was like the guy in the suspenders with the fiddle singing 'Come on, Eileen.'"

Steve rolled his eyes. He knew Michael meant well with his MTV references from 1983, but it wasn't helping.

Michael rolled toward Steve and lay on his side, as a girlfriend would.

"Well, you know, you could tell him who you are." Michael said. Steve looked at him, his eyes turning satanic. "Oh, sorry—*were,*" Michael hastened to add.

Steve got scarily intense. "No, Michael," he said. "No, Adam can't find out about this. Do you hear me, Michael? Don't you dare say a word to him—or Rhonda."

Michael knew Steve meant business. Steve may have been "a gay," but he was a foot taller than Michael, with about fifty extra pounds of muscle to boot. The qualities that made Steve a hottie to other gay guys also enabled him to kick ass, so Michael knew better than to say anything to anyone. He promised to keep Steve's secret under wraps no matter what—not just out of friendship but also out of fear of being beaten.

Michael was lying in the same bed in Steve's bedroom the following Saturday night. Only this time Steve was not next to him—Rhonda was. She had stopped by to see her boyfriend while Steve was out gay two-stepping. All night long Rhonda had been plying Michael with questions about Steve. Why did he dump Adam? What happened? Why had his decision been so abrupt? Michael feigned confusion, trying to honor Steve's insistence that he keep mum. Growing tired of the inquisition, he sat up and heaved an exasperated sigh. Rhonda sat up too.

"I told you, I don't know," he cried. "He just said Adam isn't the one."

Rhonda knew Michael knew something that he wasn't telling her. She decided to employ a tactic that all women reserve for extreme emergencies. She knew it wasn't right to use certain powers she possessed. But she realized she was using them for the good of her friend and herself. So she decided to do it: She decided to hypnotize her boyfriend with her feminine wiles.

She stared at Michael intensely. Her pretty eyes becoming slits of magical persuasion. "Michael?" she said softly yet determinedly.

"Huh?" he replied warily.

Michael looked at Rhonda's face. Suddenly, he felt something strange come over him, as if he were falling under her spell. Rhonda opened her eyes ever so gently, hooking him in.

"Michael? Is that the whole story?" Rhonda cooed. Her face was completely motionless except for her intoxicating gaze. Michael began to lose himself.

"Well," he muttered, his pupils fixed and dilated, "there is the other thing."

Rhonda knew she had him. Her hypnotic gaze intensified. "What? What other thing, Michael?" she asked.

Michael's eyes began to cross slightly. "About Adam and Steve. It's kinda gross. I think I should tell you after dinner."

Michael began to go under, almost to the point of losing consciousness. Rhonda intensified her stare to snap him back into her reality.

"Why? What do you know, Michael?"

Michael didn't want to tell, but he could feel his mouth opening. He could feel the words bubbling up from deep inside him. He had a momentary flash of Steve's angry face telling him not to tell Rhonda or Adam who he really was. But the moment came and went. The truth of Steve's past formed into words that made their way up from Michael's belly, through his chest, passing through his throat, and onto his lips.

A few moments later Rhonda screamed.

Chapter Fourteen

Adam sat in the midnight NA meeting—Whip That Crack!—on Houston Street. This was now his recovery home group. Mary, the chairperson he had met on the night of his encounter with the twink, had recently become Adam's sponsor. Adam had claimed the "burning desire," an option available to addicts whose sobriety may be in danger if they do not get the opportunity to share.

Adam sat crying in the circle of rickety folding chairs. He had been sharing for at least five minutes—telling how his heart was breaking without Steve and how he had been dumped "in the shower"—when the doors to the meeting room burst open. Rhonda and Michael came running in, frenzied. "Steve is the go-go dancer!" Rhonda screamed, her arms flailing.

Mary and Adam stood, bewildered. Mary intercepted the two insane-acting strangers.

"Excuse me, this is a private meeting," she said.

"Silence, sober one!" Rhonda replied, shouting.

"What go-go dancer?" Adam asked.

"From Danceteria! That Hershey-squirtin' cokehead!" Rhonda screeched.

Mary was not having any of this. "Excuse me, but you are challenging our serenity," she said.

"Shut up!" Michael barked. Mary threw up her arms and sat down.

Understanding began to wash over Adam's face, which was quickly turning white. He felt the blood leave his head as he began to piece it all together.

"Wait! From the '80s? Willy Wonka?"

Suddenly, it hit him. Adam remembered the Dazzle Dancer who had pooped on him. He struggled to recall the details from that night almost twenty years ago. Slowly, the images crystallized. He remembered a certain movie that the Dazzle Dancer had made at Danceteria, which then superimposed itself over a similar move Steve had made while gay two-stepping. Adam remembered how the dancer had stressed certain consonants just as Steve did now, albeit without a Texan accent. He recalled Steve's telling him that he had wanted to be a dancer when he was young. There were millions of clues in Adam's interactions with Steve over the course of the last year. Suddenly, Steve and the Dazzle Dancer who had pooped on Adam were one and the same.

Adam dropped the Styrofoam coffee cup he had been holding. He stopped breathing, frozen, his mouth agape.

"Oh, my God! Oh, my—"

Michael slapped him, rather unnecessarily.

"Adam, listen," he said. "Steve loves you, but he can't get past the humiliation over the diarrhea thing and for turning you into some kind of gay John Belushi. That's why he broke up with you. Because he didn't know you were you until that day on the Brooklyn Bridge." Adam took this in. The twenty or so twelve-steppers attending the meeting quietly sipped their coffee. Some fetched doughnuts and sat, watching the ensuing, screaming drama playing as if it were a really gay soap opera.

"But that is crazy," Adam cried. He turned to Rhonda. "You were right. He's totally unaware for a shrink."

"I'm telling you, they're like preacher's kids," Rhonda yelled. Mary leaped to her feet like a boxer entering the ring.

"Cross-talking is not allowed," she exclaimed. Adam tried to assuage her control issues.

"Mary, please. Just sit down," he said from the corners of his mouth. Mary obliged and returned to her seat. She had popped up so many times by this point she was beginning to resemble a jack-in-the-box—or crack-in-the-box in her case.

"He's so confused, Adam," Michael said.

Adam didn't agree. He began to walk toward the exit.

"No, he's not. He's just an asshole—and a baby. He's a baby who's also an asshole!"

With that, Adam left the meeting. He dissolved into tears as he ran down the hall of the church and onto the sidewalks of New York. Rhonda and Michael followed in hot pursuit. Suddenly, Adam realized it was Saturday night. And that meant only one thing.

Nearly an hour had passed by the time Adam burst through the doors of the Big Apple Rodeo. He had run home, changed into his best country-and-western duds, and flown in a cab downtown to the weekly party held in a loft in Chelsea. Rhonda and Michael had sped to Rhonda's place and quickly thrown together country outfits. Rhonda's hair was in pigtails, and she was dressed in a skimpy prairie dress that made her look like one of the *Hee Haw* Honeys. In her overstuffed closet were some costumes for the many comedy acts she had done over the years. Rhonda found a Western shirt and hat for her boyfriend, and together they hightailed it downtown.

They caught up with Adam just as he was entering the packed two-stepping club. Rhonda grabbed Adam's arm. She knew this was huge.

"Adam, if you believe it, you can achieve it," she said. "If you dream it, you can become it." Adam could barely hear her over "Only the Good Ones Are Taken"—the song that had been playing when Steve called Adam his boyfriend for the first time. Adam took this as a sign. The universe was either laughing at him or conspiring with him to achieve something wonderful. He wasn't sure what the outcome would be, but he did know one thing: He had a choice. He may not have had a choice in his misfortune, but he had a choice about how to respond to the news about Steven Hicks. He just didn't know what the outcome would be. Not just yet.

Adam moved across the packed dance floor, looking for his ex. Dozens of gay cowboys and cowgirls paraded across the brightly lit room. Boys were gently kissing other boys the way Steve and he had once done. Girls held other girls close, never wanting to let go. *All this romantic stuff is just bullshit,* Adam thought. He imagined all these lovebirds would eventually discover that the objects of their affection were not who they seemed to be at first. And once the real identities were exposed, the couples would break up, just like Steve and him.

These cynical thoughts were floating around Adam's head like a noisy halo when he spied Steve, who was slow-dancing with none other than Andy—the insanely hot, backflipping dance instructor Adam had met at the rodeo before. Steve looked up, and his face dropped when he saw Adam. He was busted. Andy stopped dancing, took in the situation, and laid his hand on Steve's shoulder territorially. Adam seethed at Andy's stupid, smug expression. A wellspring of righteous indignation bubbled up inside his belly, and he stepped forward and shoved Andy off Steve.

Suddenly, the grating sound of a record scratching reverberated across the dance hall. The music stopped, and all eyes turned to watch the imminent catfight. Adam's fur was raised, as was Andy's. Adam didn't know what to do next. He hadn't planned anything; he just knew he had to express his anger and his feelings of betrayal. He glanced over at Rhonda and Michael, who were holding on to each other in affection and fright. They stared at Adam, wondering what he would do next. They blinked back at him in mute concern.

Behind Rhonda and Michael, Adam saw a drag queen on a small stage. It was Jackie Beat, a well-known downtown chanteuse who was dressed as Dolly Parton. All gay men know that drag queens possess magical powers. They know that drag queens are the shamans of the gay community. They started the riots at Stonewall; they have turned righteous indignation into an art form. When Adam saw Jackie, she saw him. She understood what it meant to be betrayed and cast aside, especially romantically. Once Adam and she had established an unspoken understanding, she knew what needed to be done. She nodded at Adam as if to say, "You go, girl."

Thus fortified, Adam turned back to Steve and Andy and made a choice: not to punch them out, not to call them names. Adam Bernstein, the gay Jew cowboy, decided to dance. He began stomping to an imaginary beat, which would inspire the other Beat—Jackie—to conspire alongside him. Adam began to stomp in anger and noticed a particularly hot cowboy standing in the sidelines. He reached over and pulled the lad close to him. Jackie grabbed the microphone and began wailing out a song she was making up on the spot as the live band joined in freestyle.

Adam stopped stomping and started dancing like a pro as an astonished Steve watched in total astonishment. Adam swung his partner to and fro, round and round, and do-si-do. The performance culminated in a seductive bump-and-grind that made Steve's jealous blood boil.

Steve grabbed the strapping Andy and struck a pose. On the next bar of the song, it was their turn. Steve twirled the accomplished Andy around the dance floor, this time with Adam and his cowboy watching. Rhonda and Michael stood on the sidelines with the other patrons, watching the beginnings of some kind of a battle—a battle dance, if you will. Gay cowboys and cowgirls began to take sides, caught up in the drama. The Battle of the Bottoms was on.

Most of the dancers automatically sided with Andy, because he was the star of the gay rodeo. A few disenfranchised anarchists positioned themselves behind Adam in support of the underdog. Andy's status may have been akin to that of the most popular girl in high school, but like most popular girls, he had abused his position more than once. Andy was used to getting what he wanted. Maybe it was because he was blond—or because he was six foot two and ripped from head to toe. You could have served margaritas on Andy's bubble butt.

Steve twirled Andy around in a breakneck sort of swing dancing. Adam studied their moves, intent on one-upping them. He was full of rage, not just from his breakup with Steve but also from years of allowing himself to be victimized by life. He completely forgot he couldn't dance. There was no time for that sort of nonsense tonight. Steve and Andy moved across the dance floor, commanding attention and plenty of hooting and hollering from the onlookers on their side. Steve stopped dancing and stood glowering at the cowboy partnered with Adam. Andy sensed the tide turning against him. He slid down to the floor suggestively, doing the splits, putting his hands on Steve's hips and positioning his face suggestively in front of Steve's crotch. He snapped his head to punctuate his sexy move, throwing the metaphorical baton back to Adam and the cowboy.

Adam grabbed his partner. They launched into a coun-trified swing dance as Jackie Beat wailed and moaned through her song onstage. Adam knew they had to top what Steve and Andy had done. Frenzied and caught up in the emotion, the cowboy picked up Adam and flipped him upside down. Adam landed on his feet triumphantly, enormously pleased with himself, as if he did this sort of thing everyday. Then Adam threw the dance over to Andy and Steve.

Suddenly, the guys standing behind Steve and Andy seemed to fall under a magical spell that allowed them all to do the same synchronized dance moves. The twenty strapping men dipped and kicked, their boots clackety-clacking in unison on the hardwood floor. They moved toward Adam's team, which consisted of just a few brave-hearted souls. The encroaching wall of hot dancers was an intimidating sight, but Adam's team stood their ground. After one big stomp, Andy threw the dance back to Adam.

A frenzy overtook the gay Jew. Adam spun himself across the dance floor, twirling to and fro like Chita Rivera on moonshine. The other gay men on his side of the room joined in; his enthusiasm was contagious. Adam was the little engine who could, and his cowboy conductor looped him around and swung Adam threw his legs. Adam slid to a grand finale, his leg pointed like a ballerina and his arm flamboyantly poised in the air.

Jackie Beat's singing shifted into a fevered country rap and the dancers followed her lead. Very quickly the battle dance devolved into madcap whirlwind of spontaneity and showboating. Gay cowboys flung each other in the air; lesbians slapped their knees and did a jig. The Big Apple Rodeo was beginning to look like a huge gay popcorn machine. Adam and Andy continued to battle-dance with their partners, with Adam riding his cowboy like a bucking bronco across the hall. Adam removed his hat and hooted all the way. After jumping off, he danced a few moves over to the huffin' and hoofin' Steve.

"Not bad for a Dazzle Dancer," Adam said as he snapped his fingers like a sassy black girl. He danced away, leaving this bomb sitting in the middle of the floor. Steve was furious that Adam had found out the truth. He looked over at Michael, who was slapping his knee on the sidelines. He thought of going over and ripping off Michael's head, but there was no time—Adam's team was beginning to win, and some of Andy's dancers had begun to trickle over to the other side.

Adam felt his heart soar as more dancers came to his side. Andy began to panic as everyone left his area of the dance floor to back up Adam, who had begun to do a sort of chicken-fried version of the kick-ball-change.

Eventually, all the dancers were dancing behind a triumphant Adam, who kept doing his lucky dance move while Andy looked scared and confused. Suddenly, Andy got an idea. He would unleash his very own secret weapon—his infamous backflips. Seeing that the crowd had emptied from his side of the room, Andy took a deep breath and threw his legs in the air—something he was very good at indeed. He cartwheeled backward across the large loft space. Everyone watched as he demonstrated Olympic-quality gymnastics for the crowd.

Adam knew this was it. This would decide the winner of the Battle Dance. Adam spied two large, entirely decorative bales of hay near the wall behind him. Without pausing for reflection, he ran to the bales and quickly climbed to the top, standing high above the dancers. He took off his hat and threw it in the air toward the middle of the room. All the dancers, including Rhonda and Michael, dashed to form two lines in front of him. Adam swan-dived into their arms, and they flipped him up and down until he landed on his feet. Then Adam did not one, not two, but three Gay Games–inspired backflips that were even better than Andy's. He landed square on his feet, barely discombobulated, just in time to catch his falling cowboy hat.

Adam placed the hat squarely on his head, and the crowd went wild. Nobody could believe this little pip-squeak had defeated the queeny goliath of the gay rodeo. Everyone hooted and hollered and surrounded Adam as a conquering hero. Andy slinked away hat in hand, tail between his legs.

Adam had won. He looked at Steve, thanked his friends old and new, and ran out the exit. He had made his point.

Somewhere between backflips and two-stepping, he had become a man. Adam Bernstein had danced his way into adulthood on a chilly spring night in Chelsea.

Steve burst through the lobby of the building that housed the Big Apple Rodeo, looking frantically for Adam. He saw him running north and desperately followed him. He caught up with Adam at the south end of Times Square. It was late at night, so there were very few souls at the "Crossroads of the World." A few tourists and night owls strolling along Broadway noticed that two cowboys in hats and boots were having a lovers' quarrel. Steve trotted alongside Adam, trying to make him stop but to no avail.

"Adam, wait! I'm sorry, okay?" Steve pleaded.

Adam slowed his pace but didn't look at Steve. "I have nothing to say to you," he declared.

Steve followed doggedly a few more steps and then said, "I feel like I'd created this cocaine monster and unleashed him onto the gay community to wreak havoc on mimes."

Adam turned and confronted him. "Don't you mean *Rex Havoc*? That was my goth name after all."

Adam turned and walked on. Steve was fed up. He jumped in front of Adam and blocked his path.

"Look, you told me you lost everything after meeting me that night. I gave you your first bump of coke. I became…incontinent…in front of you." Steve buried his face in his hands as shame overwhelmed him.

"'Became incontinent?'" Adam sneered. "God, you are such an old lady. You're just embarrassed."

Steve looked squarely at Adam. "Yes. Yes, I am," he said. "I'd like to course through life with a lover who thought I never went to the bathroom at all, who thought a little dove came along and swept it all away when I wasn't looking."

"Everybody poops. Who gives a shit?" Adam exclaimed. He had enough of this and began to walk away, exasperated, when Steve grabbed his arm. Adam spun around and lashed out at him. "What? *What* do you want?"

"I don't know, okay? I don't want some open relationship like all the other gay couples I see. I don't want some gay version of all the straight couples I know. I don't see what I want anywhere."

Steve's honesty got to Adam, and he softened. Adam understood this dilemma. Suddenly, the problems they had seemed so much larger than they were as individuals. For the first time, Adam saw Steve not as his ex-boyfriend but as just another gay guy trying to find love in this crazy world. Adam realized he still loved Steve and wanted him back. In spite of everything that had happened, he realized that Steve was the way he was because of millions of variables, but mostly because he hadn't had any role models to help him find his way. Neither of them had been able to benefit from having healthy role models.

"Then just see…*me*," Adam implored. He took off his hat and stepped toward Steve, whose eyes were full of tears. "We're just us, you know? We're not gay or straight or Julia or Meg. We're just two *people*—Adam and Steve." Adam smiled knowingly, pleadingly.

But Steve wasn't moved. There was a long pause between them as late-night cabs whizzed by, their honking horns providing an unsettling urban soundtrack to the very urban dilemma these two gay men faced.

"Maybe we should just admit that neither of those people are relationship material," Steve said. "They're both too damaged."

Adam got his answer. His blood boiled at Steve's defeatism. He put his hat back on.

"We're in our thirties. Of course we're damaged," Adam stated matter-of-factly. "And you know what? I'm tired. I'm tired of fighting you and the whole world just so I can have something as radical and subversive as a fucking boyfriend."

Steve was stunned. He had never seen Adam so infuriated. "Fuck you, Steve! I may be damaged goods, but I am goods nonetheless!"

With that, Adam stormed across Times Square, into the city, and out of Steve Hicks's life.

Steve stood alone in the middle of the world, surrounded by lights and cars and monuments to excess.

Chapter Fifteen

When Steve got home that night, his feet hurt almost as much as his head. With Michael wisely encamped at Rhonda's, Steve's loft felt cavernous and unwelcoming. He looked across Grove Street and saw the offensive homophobe sitting in his well-lit living room drinking a beer and watching TV. A woman sat on the couch next to him. Steve watched them being affectionate with each other, something that seemed the most natural thing in the world—for them. It seemed that even the homophobe had managed to find someone dumb enough to love him.

Steve thought of yelling at them to disrupt their moment of intimacy with epithets like "breeders!" or perhaps "vagina muncher!" but he practiced restraint. Steve wondered how it could be that no gay man or lesbian had ever gone on a straight-guy murder spree. Steve wished he had the courage to take out thirty-six years of oppression on the oppressor. As he sat on his couch, exasperated, he wondered how he would do it. Maybe he could walk into a Promise Keepers meeting and open fire. But, like most gay men and lesbians, Steve knew this wouldn't ultimately help the appeal for acceptance. He wondered if he would ever be strong enough to fight for something like love—to have the strength Adam seemed to have discovered in himself. As spaced-out as Adam was, he stood up for himself. Steve knew he couldn't even yell across the street to defend his lover from horrible insults. He had never felt more like a coward. He slept in his clothes—he was too depressed and disgusted with himself to be naked, even by himself.

When Michael came home the next day, he knew he was in for it. At the same time, he wasn't sorry about blowing Steve's cover. Michael disapproved of what Steve had done to Adam—the way he had simply abandoned someone he professed to love. Whether Adam and Steve were meant to stay together was beside the point. Michael just didn't like how Steve had flipped off his heart like a light switch.

Michael was thankful Steve was absent. He was hoping Steve would be at work, although he wasn't sure. Even after five years of living together, Michael was barely aware of Steve's work schedule. Because he never worked, he just never paid attention to what day it was.

As the afternoon slid into night, Michael braced himself. He decided to clean up the apartment as a form of penance for opening his big mouth. He swept, dusted, and washed the blanket he'd used, which was stained with drool and spilled bong water. He used the DustBuster to suck up remnants of ancient Doritos crumbs from under the sectional that had until recently defined his tiny world. Since he had met Rhonda, Michael's world had expanded tenfold. He actually left the house now, spending much of his time at his girlfriend's apartment. Rhonda had had a profound effect on Michael. Her burgeoning love for him had transformed the socially inept porn addict into some semblance of an actual romantic. Adam had done the same for Steve—for a while. Michael considered this as he cleaned. He finished up and sat on the couch, waiting for the door to open and the inevitable confrontation.

Finally, Michael heard the key enter the lock. He sat on the couch, frozen, his back stiff and upright, as if his mommy or daddy were about to enter.

Steve came through the door, his lab coat in his hand. He was in his work drag—slacks, white button-down shirt, and a tie—but it was obvious he had not slept much. His hair was messy, and he had stubble on his handsome face. He entered the living room and paced like a caged animal, his eyes boring holes into his puny friend. He threw his lab coat at Michael, who waved it off with his hand as it flew toward his face.

"It's not my fault," Michael cried. "She's a woman—they have their ways."

"Oh, really? I supposed she hypnotized you with her feminine wiles?"

Michael was shocked. How could Steve have known?

"Well, yes. Yes, she did, actually!" he shrieked.

Steve glared at Michael. He knew none of this was Michael's fault. He let out a big sigh, then slowly moved to the couch, and sat at the end opposite his roommate.

"What?" Steve exclaimed. "What was I supposed to do, Michael? Every time he'd go to an AA meeting, I'd feel guilty. Every time I'd use the bathroom, he'd stare at me with a knowing look on his face."

Michael rolled his eyes. "Oh, please. Get over yourself," he said. "The guy saw you take a dump. You'd eventually start changing each other's diapers anyway."

Steve ran his fingers through his hair exasperatedly. He pulled on his tie and loosened it. "This is not how it's supposed to be, Michael," he said.

Michael tried to regain Steve's attention. "Listen, you've got to stop with all that preconceived bullshit. You guys love each other, don't you?" he asked imploringly.

Steve's eyes welled with emotion. His vision became blurred from the tears filling his eyes. "I don't even know what that is anymore," he said.

Steve broke down crying, and he put his face in his hands. This was huge. Steve had not cried in nearly thirty years, and for thirty years the universe had been conspiring to get him to cry again. Michael sat watching this grown man—the husband in his sexless, codependent marriage—weep into his own helpless hands. Having no experience with emotion—his or anyone else's—Michael was at a loss. He wondered what the appropriate thing would be to do. He had learned everything he knew about life through cable television. It seemed that when people cried on TV, the person they were with always touched them to show support. Michael stood, approached the despondent Steve, and sat next to him. Then he lifted his left arm and tentatively—oh, so tentatively—laid his hand on Steve's shoulder. The fact that Michael lived with a gay guy was one thing. The fact that he was actually touching that gay guy was another thing entirely. As he sat there, his hand patting Steve on the shoulder supportively, he thanked God that no one could see them. If he had to touch a gay guy, at least it would be in private. Like a tree that falls in the forest and doesn't make a noise, this act of straight-gay brotherhood would be contained in the privacy of their own—

"Fags!" brayed the voice from across the street.

Michael retracted his hand faster than you can say, well, "fag." Across the street, the homophobe stood on his balcony and peered into the loft. His female companion had apparently left, which freed him up to do really important things like harass his neighbors.

Steve's tears turned into a quietly burning rage. Michael looked up at the hate-filled heterosexual across the way. He wanted to declare, "I'm not gay—I'm just nice." But it was no use.

"God made Adam and Eve, not Adam and Steve!" the homophobe shouted. The words echoed not only across Grove Street but also in the walls of Steve's foggy head. Suddenly, Steve bolted up from the sofa. His eyes locked onto the homophobe in a violent, determined way. In that moment Steve had a much-needed epiphany. He grabbed his keys and stormed out of the apartment, slamming the door and leaving a completely confused Michael staring up at the redheaded monster across the street.

Downstairs at Marie's Crisis piano bar, Rhonda was in the weeds. For some reason unknown to her, the bar's happy hour was unusually packed with thirsty musical-theater lovers that day. Sitting at the bar was someone who was anything but happy. Adam gripped his Diet Coke for dear life. Even though he had triumphed at the Battle Dance the night before, his glory was unbelievably fleeting. When Adam had woken up that morning, the full impact of losing Steve had hit him. His heart was desperately broken. He finally understood what having a broken heart meant—it was as if there were an actually hole in his chest; it hurt *physically.* Adam had never felt this kind of intense inner pain, and it was nearly unbearable.

Worried for her friend and unable to get Maggie, the other waitress, to sub, Rhonda had forced Adam to come with her to work. She didn't want him to be alone. She knew all about Adam's alcoholism and had some reservations about bringing him to a bar, but Marie's wasn't just a bar. It was a magical place they had found together several years ago, right after the terrorist attacks of 9/11, which was the last time she had seen Adam this blue. Walking home arm in arm after a candlelit vigil and thoroughly depressed by the state of the world, they had heard—*singing!*—coming from the basement of a charming old building. Spellbound, Rhonda and Adam entered Marie's hundred-year-old walls, and for the first time in days they laughed and smiled while singing Broadway show tunes with other New Yorkers seeking a much-needed catharsis. That night, they all sang songs like "New York, New York," and everyone cried and hugged total strangers. Rhonda wanted more of this in her life and eventually landed a job at Marie's as a cocktail waitress. The money sucked, but she didn't care—she needed this place. And that night Adam needed Rhonda.

The former fat goth girl Maura Bid approached her morbid best friend, who sat at the bar leaning on his elbow, lost in thought.

"I gotta go get limes, honey. Be right back," she said.

Adam didn't answer. He barely heard her. When Rhonda put down her serving tray and scurried out the door, Adam finally looked up. Across from him was the most beautiful display of every kind of liquor known to humankind—or at least to theater queens. Adam's mouth began to water. He could taste the whiskey, the brandy, the rum, and tequila. He imagined them going down his throat and the warm glow that would follow. He imagined how the alcohol would make him feel different than the way he felt. He had been sober for over a year and a half now. It had been a long time since he touched alcohol—he knew that his system was so pure, he would really feel its effect. This is the challenge for the clean and sober person—the first drink of a relapse provides a lot of ecstasy. Adam was triggered. He started to wonder if he really was an alcoholic. Maybe he had gotten so fucked up for other reasons. Maybe he could drink again like a normal person. And for a gay geek alcoholic who couldn't seem to find true love, the notion of normal was very attractive. He couldn't lose the label of gay or Jew or misanthrope, but he could lose the label of recovering drunk, and one less label in life couldn't hurt.

As Rhonda headed to the deli at the corner, she paused to see if she had money on her. Suddenly, from above she heard what sounded like a loud explosion. A million pieces of shattered glass rained down onto Grove Street. Thinking perhaps terrorists had decided to attack gay piano bars, Rhonda glanced up to see what appeared to be a man pulling another man out of the window facing Steve's building. They were both screaming at each other, grunting and growling. Loud, antigay, hateful slurs echoed across the street, along with sounds of fists punching faces and clothing being ripped. Rhonda crossed the street to get a better view. Suddenly, she realized that the man reaching into the apartment was none other than Steve.

Rhonda covered her mouth to repress a scream, and Michael emerged from the building across the street, eyes pointed upward toward the melee just as Steve successfully removed the homophobe from his apartment. Rhonda and Michael looked at each other and got an idea.

Inside Marie's, Adam had made a choice. No longer at the whim of fate, he made a conscious choice to no longer feel the feelings he was experiencing. He just wanted to feel comfortable in his own skin. Steve had helped him feel that way, but Adam's thin skin, which had helped him to be open and intimate in a love relationship, did not serve him while he was alone. The things that made him lovable to Steve were also the qualities that made it difficult for him to navigate the superficial gay dating scene.

Adam pushed his Diet Coke away and replaced it with an empty shot glass. He then reached over and pulled a bottle of Dewar's close. Hands trembling, he poured himself a nice big alcoholic drink. He sat huddled at the bar, looking at the whiskey for a moment while revelers sang a popular Broadway show tune behind him. Slowly, he raised the shot glass to his mouth. Fluttering inside his stomach were the butterflies of conscience, which would soon be drowned by the scalding effects of alcohol. As the glass approached his lips, Adam suddenly noticed that the music and singing had stopped. He felt eyes on his back and turned around.

Standing in the middle of the bar was Steve—battered, bruised, and bloody. His clothes were torn, and his face was covered with scrapes and dirt. Steve was gripping the homophobe—using all his might to control the squirming bigot, who also appeared pretty beat-up in a ripped T-shirt and acid-washed jeans from the '80s. It was obvious that Steve had punched this man square in the nose, which looked as red as his curly, short hair. Rhonda and Michael stood just behind Steve and his captive, their faces frozen into a portrait of determination.

Adam sat at the bar on his stool, looking confusedly at Steve and the homophobe.

"Hi," Steve said.

"Hi," Adam replied.

"Um, this is Charlie. He lives across the street from me."

When Adam realized that Charlie was the homophobe, his jaw dropped in astonishment.

"Oh. Hi," Adam murmured.

"Hi," Charlie squeaked. Steve had Charlie's arms pinned behind his back.

"Okay, now ask him. *Ask him!*" Steve growled. He tightened his grip on Charlie, who shouted in pain.

"What's your name?" Charlie asked the man sitting on the stool.

"Adam."

"That's right. And what's mine?" Steve asked Charlie.

"Steve," Charlie said, rolling his eyes.

"That's right—Adam and Steve. So you see, you were wrong. God did make Adam and Steve because *here we are!*" Steve violently yanked Charlie's arm behind his back even farther, causing Charlie to yelp. "Okay, now what else? *What else?*"

Charlie submitted to Steve's wishes. Again he addressed Adam: "Steve is sorry for the way he treated you. He's sorry about everything."

Adam realized that Steve was using this asshole from across the street to do his apologizing for him. While Adam was impressed at the lengths Steve was going to make his point, it still wasn't coming from his own lips. It seemed to Adam that once again Steve wasn't willing to own up to his own shit, so to speak.

"Well, I accept his apology," Adam stated coolly. He was careful not to give in to Steve's manipulation.

Nevertheless, Steve persisted. "*And...*" he said. He pulled Charlie's arm tighter. The words seemed to be getting squeezed out of this man like verbal toothpaste.

"I'm sorry that I yelled at ya, called ya cornholers in front of his parents," Charlie moaned.

"Okay," Adam said. He was getting tired of this display. The last thing he wanted was to be talking to this guy.

Still, Steve choked more words out of Charlie. "And he wants to ask you for your hand in one of them gay marriages."

Adam took this in. He stood and approached the middle of the bar, where Steve and Charlie stood.

"A man marry a man? That's kind of gross," Adam said sarcastically, his arms crossing as he approached the sweaty homophobe.

"I know," Charlie said.

"Well, you tell him that personally I don't really believe in marriage. And I don't know if I believe in him anymore."

Steve's face dropped. So did Charlie's.

"Whoa! That's harsh," Charlie cracked. Steve pushed him away and stood alone, facing Adam. Rhonda and Michael stood watching them watch each other, as did the rest of the patrons in the bar.

"Adam, please," Steve said.

Adam's insides were a jumble of emotion. On one hand, he wanted to jump into this man's arms—the man he loved so dearly. On the other hand, he wanted to protect himself from further injury. He also wanted to punish Steve for abandoning him, and the best way to do that would be not to give Steve what he wanted in that moment. But Adam wondered if by rejecting Steve he was really rejecting himself. All these thoughts swam in the gulf that occupied the space between them.

"I can't," Adam said, conflicted.

"Adam, I choose you." Steve stepped forward and put both hands on Adam's upper arms. "I choose *you.*"

Adam looked at the floor, avoiding Steve's intense gaze.

"Well, I don't know why you would," Adam whispered.

Steve glanced at the bar behind Adam. He saw the shot glass filled with whiskey and realized that Adam was in a very hopeless place. It all made sense. He had to do something. He may have given Adam his first bump of coke, but tonight he could save him from the first drink of a relapse.

Steve recalled the night they met in 1987. He needed Adam to understand that he acknowledged the past, that he owned up to it. So he decided to do something he had done that fateful night. He sang.

> Perhaps I had a wicked childhood.
> Perhaps I had a miserable youth.
> But somewhere in my wicked, miserable past,
> there must have been a moment of truth.

Adam looked at Steve as if he were insane. Rhonda put her hand over her face to shield herself from the sight of Steve's very public embarrassment. Michael also thought Steve might be blowing it. But Adam wasn't so sure. The man he loved was singing to him. *Singing!*

Steve finished his serenade and looked at Adam imploringly. He was spent. He had given his all to this man in this moment. Adam's eyes were filled with tears. Suddenly, there was a loud sob near them. Everyone turned and saw the homophobe Charlie with tears streaming down his face; he was enormously moved. Adam turned back to Steve, took a breath, and collapsed into his arms. Steve smiled and stroked Adam's hair as Adam cried on his shoulder. They held each other very tight, never to part again, as the crowd burst into spontaneous applause. Rhonda and Michael also held each other, like the good codependent friends they were. The piano player wisely launched into an upbeat tune from *Funny Girl*—Rhonda's and Michael's favorite—and the music and singing gradually drowned out the clapping.

Adam disentangled himself from Steve, walked over to the bar, and gave the shot of whiskey to Michael. Even though he wouldn't be drinking it, the thought of pouring good booze down a drain was unacceptable to an alcoholic—even a sober one. Steve's love had saved him from a relapse, but Adam knew he had saved Steve too. *Sometimes people save each other from themselves,* he thought. *This is why people love.*

Chapter Sixteen

Adam stood before the shatterproof full-length mirror at his parents' house. Dressed in a brand-new tuxedo, his hair slicked back, he thought of all the times he had dressed in black as a teen in this very room, the room he had grown up in. He slowly moved around the bedroom, looking at all the evidence of his life. *Star Wars* memorabilia, Robert Smith memorabilia, an old portable eight-track player—all these things reminded Adam of who he really was.

Adam had realized he was gay in this room around age thirteen. At the time he hadn't thought, *Wow, someday I'll grow up and become a cocaine addict who sleeps with mimes.* Instead, he had thought, *Wow, someday I'll have a boyfriend.* It had taken him over twenty-five years to remember who he had been before life had told him to be someone else. Like most gay men, he had started out a romantic. And like most gay men, Steve included, Adam had lapsed into the promiscuity of the *failed* romantic.

As Adam sat on the bed musing about all this, his mother peeked her head in.

"Hi, honey. Ready for the big day?"

Adam smiled and nodded. His mom had recently had

her headgear removed. In fact, ever since the news of Adam and Steve's engagement, the Bernstein curse had seemingly vanished. Both Adam's sister and mother had been accident-free for the most part. This had been a revelation to both women. Unencumbered by casts or braces of any kind, Sherry and Ruth had gone on a long-overdo shopping spree, splurging on blouses and skirts that didn't have to accommodate any handicaps.

Ruth had been particularly excited about Adam's wedding. Ruth had always lived through her big brother to some degree and she thought Steve was, like, *totally* hot. Adam's success in love didn't make her jealous; instead it inspired her. Perhaps she might also find the love of her life. If Adam could turn his luck around, maybe she had a chance too.

Sherry sat on the bed next to her son and held his hand. "I am so proud of you," she said.

Adam looked at his mom, who was dressed in a pretty blue dress. She had gotten her hair done for the wedding and looked wonderful. Sherry had given birth to Adam when she was only nineteen, and because of their relative closeness in age they had become good friends as adults.

"Thanks, Mom," Adam said. "Is everything okay out there? Are the guests arriving?"

"Oh, yes. They're getting acquainted in back and everything's fine, although there is this little Chinese girl who threw a plate at your friend Rhonda."

Adam's and Steve's wedding was about to take place in the ample backyard of the Bernsteins' Long Island home. Traditionally, the bride's family is supposed to pay for and stage the wedding. This fact proved to be a major topic of discussion for Adam and Steve. Whose parents were the bride's when two men were going to be united? Consideration of who was more the top and who was more the bottom quickly dissolved into icky territory. Adam's people lived nearby on Long Island and were completely free of homophobia, so it was decided that the Bernsteins should put on the wedding—which they greeted with unbridled enthusiasm. Adam and his mother had tended to the invitations, picked out a cake, and chosen the clergyperson: Adam's AA sponsor, Mary.

Mary may have been a bipolar crack addict who was now just bipolar, but she was also an ordained New Age minister who was able to marry people. Because she had been watching Adam mature into his sobriety in various recovery groups, she also felt she'd had a hand in helping him find his way to this point in his life.

As Adam and Sherry sat together and talked about the details of what was going on outside his bedroom door, there was a knock.

"Hey, it's me," Steve said through the door. "Can I come in?"

Sherry jumped to her feet and held the door shut.

"No. It's bad luck to see, uh, the groom before the wedding."

Outside the door Steve smiled.

"Oh, right, gotcha. Well, please tell the groom that the other groom can't wait to start the rest of his life with him."

Steve walked away from Adam's bedroom, down the hall, and into the backyard, where around fifty guests milled about happily. Michael—dressed in jeans, high-tops, and a jacket and tie—stood near the buffet table with Rhonda, who was eyeing the many items she couldn't eat. In the center of the yard were numerous folding white chairs that faced a gazebo covered in flowers where the nuptials would take place. Adam's friends from AA were all there, sipping sparkling apple cider. Steve's upwardly mobile friends were drinking the hard stuff.

Ruth sat with her wheelchair-bound father and petted Burt, who had a red bow tie around his neck. As Steve took all this in, he wondered if his parents would come. He had begged them to come. He had even offered to pay for their airfare from Texas, but as of the night before they still weren't sure if they could handle seeing their only son marry another man and *kiss* him in front of an audience. Dottie had promised Steve she would talk to his father, but secretly Steve held little hope of their attending. So many times he had longed for their approval and support, but he also understood the psychology that prevented them from giving him what he wanted.

Mary moved through the crowd dressed in flowing gold garb. "Everyone take your places," she announced. "It's about to start."

With that, the wedding guests all moved to their seats. Even though there had been a rehearsal the night before, Steve was unbelievably nervous. Rhonda and Norm stood with Adam near the backdoor, waiting in the wings for the procession to begin. Steve and Michael, his best man, stood at the altar with Mary and faced the crowd.

Rhonda and Adam held hands as the wedding march began outside. She lifted a single white rose gently to her nose, inhaling the beauty of this day. She wouldn't be losing a best friend; she'd be gaining another. She touched Adam's face and walked outside into the lush greenery, down the aisle separating the two sides, and toward Mary.

As the music swelled everyone stood and looked toward the house as Adam emerged with his father, who scooted beside him down the aisle and gave him away at the altar. Fifteen minutes later the wedding was underway. Mary faced the crowd while Adam faced Steve and Rhonda faced Michael.

"Friends and family, at this point in the proceedings, we like to do the ring ceremony. Rhonda, if you could give me Adam's ring for Steve."

Rhonda reached over and presented the simple gold band to Mary. Adam had spent virtually all of his modest savings on the wedding band for his lover. Mary thanked Rhonda, then turned to the short man standing across from her.

"Michael, if you could give me Steve's ring for Adam." Michael reached into his pocket and, after fingering through old cigarette butts and remnants of Cheetos, removed Steve's ring from Tiffany's. He handed it to Mary, then slapped his best friend on the back, the way straight guys do.

Mary held the rings together in her hands, which were clasped together as if in prayer. She raised them skyward.

"Father-Mother God, we come to you right now to ask for your blessings on these beautiful wedding rings for Adam and Steve so they may find in their union health and happiness, peace and joy, and unconditional loving for each other. So be it."

Adam and Steve stood facing each other, transfixed and recording every moment of this experience. Mary turned to her right and handed Adam the band Rhonda had given her.

"Adam, if you could please repeat after me: 'Steve, with this ring, I thee wed.'"

Adam took Steve's large, manly hand into his own. He slipped the ring onto Steve's finger and repeated Mary's words tenderly. She handed Steve his ring for Adam and asked him to speak the same vow. Steve took Adam's smaller hand into his own, and his gaze was warm and intense.

"Adam, with this ring, I thee wed," he said.

Adam and Steve held hands as Mary continued.

"Adam Bernstein, do you take Steven Hicks to be your beloved husband?"

Adam finally cracked a smile. "I do," he said.

"Steven Hicks, do you take Adam Bernstein to be your beloved husband?"

"You bet your ass I do!" he exclaimed.

Mary and everyone else chucked at Steve's enthusiastic response.

"And now, by the power vested in me by the state of New York, I now pronounce you husband and husband. You may kiss your beloved."

With that, Adam and Steve leaned into each other and kissed each other gently and warmly with true love and affection. As they pulled away they turned to the audience. Steve gasped when he saw Dottie and Joe sitting in the front row. Steve's eyes filled with tears when he saw that his parents were not only there but also beaming with happiness. Dottie waved, then put her hands to her face to contain her emotion.

Steve turned back to Adam, who had also noticed Dottie and Joe. Adam understood the importance of this for his new husband. He smiled knowingly and nodded.

"Now, Adam, in the tradition of your family, we will break the glass," Mary said.

At Adam's and Steve's feet lay a glass wrapped in cloth. Adam raised his leg and stomped down on the package, fulfilling the Jewish tradition.

"Mazel tov!" Mary exclaimed excitedly. She raised her arms skyward to signal the end of the ceremony.

The crowd erupted into loud, fervent applause as Adam and Steve were presented to the world. Norm Bernstein clapped the loudest from his wheelchair. After all these years of bad luck, one of his children had found true happiness. Overcome with joy, Norm realized the feeling in his lower body had returned, and he leaped to his feet, jumping up and down and clapping loudly. At that moment Sherry screamed, realizing that gay love had cured her husband's paralysis. Adam and Ruth looked at each other and silently bade farewell to the last vestiges of the Bernstein curse.

Adam laughed at the wonderment of it all just as Steve swept him up into his arms. Steve marched back down the aisle, cradling Adam. Michael, Rhonda, and Mary followed giddily. Norm sat in Sherry's chair and pulled her onto his lap aggressively. She sat there laughing like a schoolgirl.

As Adam walked around the reception after his gay wedding, he felt like a camera recording the movie of his life. He observed the various kooks who occupied his world. Two families had given birth to two boys destined to find each other in a world that did not want them to fall in love.

As he moved slowly, taking in the smiling faces through the lens of his mind's eye, he wondered what a movie about Steve and him would look like. Certainly, big Hollywood stars would play them—most likely, straight actors showing the world how brave they were. Worse still, a movie about their romance might not even be about two men. Perhaps it would be reconceived as *Adam & Eve,* and either Julia Roberts or Meg Ryan would be the one with really bad luck. But as Adam walked toward a beaming Steve, he realized he didn't really believe in luck anymore. Only love.